Shadows in the Wind

Edward L. Ziola

USA • Canada • UK • Ireland

© Copyright 2006 Edward L. Ziola.
All rights reserved. No part of this publication may be reproduced, stored in a retrieval system, or transmitted, in any form or by any means, electronic, mechanical, photocopying, recording, or otherwise, without the written prior permission of the author.

Cover Design: Darlene Nickull, Kamloops, BC
Editor: Audrey McClellan, Victoria, BC

Note for Librarians: A cataloguing record for this book is available from Library and Archives Canada at www.collectionscanada.ca/amicus/index-e.html
ISBN 1-4120-9582-4

Printed in Victoria, BC, Canada. Printed on paper with minimum 30% recycled fibre.
Trafford's print shop runs on "green energy" from solar, wind and other environmentally-friendly power sources.

Offices in Canada, USA, Ireland and UK

Book sales for North America and international:
Trafford Publishing, 6E–2333 Government St.,
Victoria, BC V8T 4P4 CANADA
phone 250 383 6864 (toll-free 1 888 232 4444)
fax 250 383 6804; email to orders@trafford.com

Book sales in Europe:
Trafford Publishing (UK) Limited, 9 Park End Street, 2nd Floor
Oxford, UK OX1 1HH UNITED KINGDOM
phone 44 (0)1865 722 113 (local rate 0845 230 9601)
facsimile 44 (0)1865 722 868; info.uk@trafford.com

Order online at:
trafford.com/06-1337

10 9 8 7 6 5 4 3 2

DEDICATION

I would like to dedicate this book to the memory of my parents, Cyril and Florence Ziola. They emigrated from their native Poland to Canada in the late 1920s with high hopes for a better life in this land of plenty, only to find that they had arrived just in time for the Great Depression. Times, no doubt, were hard, but they persevered and raised a family of nine children on a hardscrabble farm in Manitoba. It is only in the years since I left that little prairie farm of my childhood that I realize the caliber of people that they were. Although, perhaps, they did not make a great financial success of their endeavors, it is the values that they passed on to their children that is worthy of mention.

    They now lie at rest at Saint Henry's cemetery at Melville, Saskatchewan, and perhaps it is their headstone that says it best, "Loved by all that knew them."

CONTENTS

Introduction. 7

A Summer Wind 11

Hotel 37

Marty. 47

Yesterday's Summer 59

Andy's Star. 65

When the Wind Was Free 75

A Box of Memories. 85

A Touch of Rhubarb 111

Bury Me in Crabtree 121

A Christmas Memory. 129

A Loony Tune or A Prairie Melody 135

Night Passage. 147

Jack's Journey. 161

The Bells of St. Aubin 173

INTRODUCTION

When I toyed with the idea of writing a book of short stories with a bit of a prairie flavor, I thought that I would be documenting a fictional history of a certain area, one that holds a special place in the hearts of all who had lived their early years in the prairie region. I now realize that the stories are more indicative of a time, those years of "growing up" in a time ever so much more innocent, a time with boundless horizons and dreams of a greater tomorrow; dreams that in later years would never quite fulfill their promise.

Throughout the almost half century since I left the place of my childhood, I had seen, with some misgivings, many small towns of the prairie region shrivel and slowly fade into oblivion, leaving nothing behind but faded memories, a few weathered old buildings silvered with age, unkempt cemeteries and a haunting, almost intangible testament to a time that once was, when large families were the norm and rural areas, especially, were much more populated than they now are. In my mind I can still hear the sound of the crowd cheering on the local baseball team at a Sunday picnic on a sunny summer afternoon. I can hear the sound of the voices of the young people making their way on foot to the nearby town in anticipation of the Saturday night dance, or perhaps the sound of trace chains from the passing of a team and wagon on a nearby road. The smell of freshly baked bread emanating from the oven of a wood stove, even in the heat of a summer's day, is something that can never be duplicated. The fragrance from a far-off grass fire on a late summer afternoon when the sun hangs red in a smoky haze can, even to this day, bring a touch of nostalgia to the heart.

Much of the land lies silent now. The voices are heard no more. The all-encompassing silence that pervades the rural areas of Manitoba and Saskatchewan, as well as those diminishing little communities scattered here and there, belies the stature that they once enjoyed. The principals of the conglomerates now in charge of the stewardship of the land reside in larger towns and cities far removed from the lands in question. Only the hedgerows that surround these scattered farmsteads still hoard their treasures in the form of rusting old farm equipment and assorted knickknacks from a bygone era. They guard their secrets well. A quiet peace reigns over all.

I decided, in the writing of this book, to create some new towns. These can never die, because they never were. Many of the communities in the following stories are fictional, although the emotions and the memories are very real, enjoyed by all who spent their childhood on the prairie. Many of the prairie towns that have survived and grown with the passing of the years now boast a facade of prosperity. Paved roads and streets, fast-food outlets, big-box stores and the hustle and bustle of modern living are there for all to see. Somewhere along their journey, these towns have lost their soul. Friendship, kinship and neighborly goodwill seem to be much less prevalent today. The rapid passage of the sand in the hourglass and a feverish race for the almighty dollar rule the day.

This is why I find those towns like Spears, Love and Piapot, Saskatchewan, so dear to my heart. Although they struggle yet to maintain their identity, they are not as they once were. A stillness dwells in the scattered, vacant houses, their silent windows hung with yellowing curtains. No hand is there to draw aside the curtain. No enquiring face peers out to see who passes. Here it is pos-

INTRODUCTION

sible to feel the presence of those long-ago days, far removed from the chaos of modern times. Life was lived then by the season, not by the minute. One can still recall the emergence of a gigantic prairie moon from a distant eastern horizon while the purple afterglow of a glorious sunset lingers in the western sky. In the mind it is possible to see the flickering of the fireflies in the velvet darkness of the prairie night or to see the glow of a kerosene lamp in a kitchen window. To hear the poignant call of the whippoorwill is something that can never be forgotten. The ever-changing living sky will never cease to conjure memories: galleons of towering cumulous clouds awash in a sea of blue, spectacular lightning storms sometimes, or the occasional dreaded black funnel. Boredom is not a word suffered easily on the prairie.

So it is that I write these stories from a perspective of looking back to a time that once was. The stories are poignant, moving across the mind of the reader like shadows, shadows set into a background of that eternal prairie wind, that cleansing prairie wind that sent all the cares and anxieties of childhood tumbling, like tumbleweeds, into the distance across the endless plain.

I can truthfully say, "I remember, I remember ... I remember."

A SUMMER WIND

They had been children of the prairie, in every sense of the words. They had come into being in the great flat land, knowing, in their early years, only that never-ending expanse that seemed almost empty at times, yet teemed with the secrets of the universe when closely studied. They had been born into this life many miles apart, yet the often fickle hand of fate would decree that they should spend a short time together, only a few weeks of a now-distant summer, a summer that would, within their memories, last forever. It was a time of innocence, a time of dreams, a time to contemplate the future, a future still unknown although vividly portrayed in their imagination. The dream would always seem to be just beyond their grasp, shimmering in the golden sun, teasing in the scurrying shadows of the clouds, dancing on the glimmering surface of the puddles resulting from a sudden downpour, or simply tumbling along, with no aim or purpose, carried on a fragrant summer wind. That summer would end, as all summers do.

Thomas smiled as these thoughts passed fleetingly through his mind. Although he had remembered that special summer of 1954 many times over the ensuing years, it now seemed that the memories had faded somewhat, the result of disillusionment or old age he supposed. Yes, the memories had faded until that telephone call just two weeks before, a phone call from out of the blue, a voice from long ago. So here he was, making this journey from Vancouver to a little town on the prairie to recapture his youth of fifty years before. He drove with the driver's side window rolled down. It was a nondescript car, three years old with no special extras, just a tool he needed in his business as well as for personal use. The date was September 19, very near the official end of summer. The weather was gorgeous, with a gentle breeze, golden sunshine, golden leaves on the hillsides and the telltale strands of gossamer spider web floating through the air, heralding the end of the summer season. It was a fitting time to make this journey, at summer's end, not only in the seasons of time but of life as well. The smile seemed to fade slightly; a look of sadness touched his eyes momentarily as he pondered the last fifty years of his life.

Nineteen hundred and fifty-four arrived with the January blizzards, the icy wind moaning across the barren landscape, white as far as the eye could see, with only an occasional break in the monotony where chimney smoke rose from a distant farm house or where a lonely snow-covered spruce or a starkly naked poplar tree huddled against the onslaught of the wind. Tommy, swaddled in his heavy winter clothes, a scarf wrapped around his neck, did not seem to feel the winter's bite. After all, he had lived here on this Manitoba farm for all of his ten years. He knew that the season would change in its own good time. This year he would reach his eleventh birthday, and the summer would hold a special treat for him. Uncle Jim and Aunt Dorothy had been to the farm at Christmastime, just a week before. They made their home at Danville Junction, Saskatchewan, a town about two hundred miles distant. Uncle Jim was an elevator agent there, and he had suggested to his sister, Tommy's mother, that perhaps Tommy could spend the coming summer at their home. "It'll do him good," he intoned with a twinkle in his eye, "give him a bit of the city life, away from the farm." Tommy, now deep in thought, gazed across the barren plain, his mind conjuring up visions of a movie theater or even an honest-to-goodness ice-cream parlor.

A Summer Wind

The next five months would seem forever.

Thomas slowed the car a bit as he overtook a large transport truck. Checking fore and aft, he quickly passed the heavily laden vehicle. "Funny," he thought, "how this highway resembles so much the roadway of my life, curves, hills and hollows where you least expect them." In his own personal rearview mirror he could remember every one. It seemed like yesterday that he had left school in search of employment. Times had been different then. At sixteen years of age you might be expected to buckle down and contribute something to your keep. Usually when you left home for your first job there would be no looking back. His situation had followed that pattern, and he had worked at various jobs, eventually making his way to Vancouver Island where he had been employed in the logging industry for about fifteen years. He had come to know and love a small community on the west coast of the island. It carried the name of Jordan River. He might have been content to live out his life there, but, as luck would have it, an unseen curve in that road changed everything. To this day he could not recall the entire chain of events, only a snapping choker cable, a log hurtling through the air, a kaleidoscope of colors, then oblivion. Weeks later he had awoken in a hospital room in Vancouver, unable to move, in constant pain and wondering just what had happened. His back had been badly broken, among other things, and nine months later he had hobbled out of that hospital into a different world then that which he had known before.

Feeling the breeze rushing by his cheek through the open window of the car and savoring the glorious late summer weather, Thomas realized again how lucky he had been. Although the accident had left him a changed man, unable to pursue his former active lifestyle, he could still navigate fairly well, even three decades after the fact. He had received a settlement from the Compensation Board for his injuries and had gone in search of a way to earn a living. A small secondhand store on a secondary street in the city of Vancouver caught his fancy, and after lengthy negotiations he had bought it, using his settlement from the Compensation Board as a down payment. The sign above the door had read *New and Used Emporium*. He quickly changed it to *Jordan River Trading*. The years since, except for the first two or three when he was still learning the business, had been good, and although he had not acquired wealth from the project, he had paid for it over time and had made a fairly decent living. He had never married, and the business occupied most of his days.

"Odd how the wind of chance blows through life," thought Thomas as he glimpsed the setting sun in the rearview mirror, absently calculating that he had about an hour of daylight left before he would have to look for a motel room

He reached for his water bottle on the seat beside him, removed the cap with one hand and took a small sip. About six months ago he had bought a collection of personal items and jewelry from an estate. Some old fellow had passed on and his stepson had been disposing of his personal effects. It was an odd collection, some of good quality but nothing really noteworthy. One piece, a bracelet of some sort, appeared old and had a strange inscription engraved on its surface. It was real gold and Thomas had paid the going gold price for it. He had been a bit puzzled by it and decided to show it to a friend of his, Jerry Stark, a professor at the university. Jerry had examined the piece carefully, turning it over to see it from every angle.

"You know, I believe that inscription is ancient Egyptian. You may have something here. I think we should submit it for further study."

Well the long and short of it was that the piece had been found to be very old indeed. The sad fact was that it had been stolen years before from a Cairo museum along with several other artifacts. How it had ended up in the old fellow's estate he would never know. He never laid eyes on the stepson again. He returned the piece to its rightful owner, the museum, but the story was so intriguing that he had received several column inches in a newspaper chain right across the country. Shortly after the story was published, he arrived home one evening and opened his door to the ringing of the telephone.

"Hi, Tommy," began a woman's voice on the line. "I wonder if you remember after all these years. This is, or was, Amy Stiles."

Thomas had been momentarily struck dumb, unable to utter a sound for what seemed like an eternity, yet encompassed only a few seconds. With a catch in his voice he uttered, "Amy? Amy Stiles? From Danville Junction, Saskatchewan?"

"As ever was," came the reply, "although I haven't been Amy Stiles for almost forty years. I'm still Amy Bishop even though Conrad has been gone for five years."

A sequential train of thought raced through Thomas's mind as he recalled that Amy had moved away from Danville Junction more than forty years before. They had gone their separate ways, in pursuit of their own destiny. She had entered the nursing profession and had met and married a young doctor, Conrad Bishop, from South Africa. Shortly after, they had moved to South Africa, where he had conducted a successful practice for a number of years. Thomas had last spoken to Amy on the final day of August in 1954. All of the relevant information he had received from others over the years.

"After Conrad's passing, I decided to return home to retire. I still own the house that my mom and dad lived in, and there are still a few people here that I am close to. As you know, the South African situation is not the best these days. Imagine my surprise when I picked up the newspaper and saw your name in it."

Thomas replied, "I can't believe it's you. I still recall you standing on the station platform as I left for home on the train so many years ago. How many dreams and plans we made. I guess somewhere along the way everything changed."

Thomas recalled that conversation as the endless miles slipped by beneath his wheels. They had talked for forty-five minutes. It did not take him long to decide that he was due for a holiday. He would close up shop for a month and visit the prairie for the first time in several years. Although Amy was the only person he now knew in Danville Junction, he would make that town the first stop on his agenda.

Thomas adjusted his rearview mirror slightly to compensate for the brilliant sunset reflected within. He would stop for the night at the next town. The winding blacktop beckoned before him. The mountains had been left behind and rolling foothills now met his gaze. He had departed from the main highway, choosing instead to travel a less busy secondary route. His thoughts drifted, not along the road ahead but rather down the road behind, all those years ago.

This July day of 1954 seemed to last forever as Tommy anxiously awaited their arrival at Danville Junction. Uncle Jim had explained to him how the town got its name. It was due to the intersection nearby of the highway running south to north with the one running east to west. They were in no hurry, and it was after five o'clock in the afternoon when they pulled into their driveway. At first glance Tommy was disappointed. He had envisioned their house as being right in the center of town, but it was actually on the edge, on the last street before the town gave way to the open prairie. Looking around he saw that the railroad track ran by no more than four hundred yards away. The adjacent area was dotted with small ponds and stands of

A Summer Wind

willows. The farmland beyond the tracks stretched toward the distant horizon and appeared remote and mysterious in the late afternoon sun. After a brief inspection of the surrounding area, he quickly hurried into the house. Aunt Dorothy had promised to make a favorite dish for supper: hot dogs and fried potatoes with vanilla ice cream for dessert.

The next morning, after a satisfying breakfast of bacon and eggs, Tommy had waved goodbye as his uncle Jim had driven away to his workplace at the elevator visible in the near distance. Aunt Dorothy was busy with her morning chores. Tommy wandered into the front yard, eagerly looking about to see more of his surroundings. As his gaze passed over the adjacent picket fence, he saw a face looking back at him, blue eyes framed by a mass of golden curls.

"Hi, I'm Amy."

He walked to the fence and, looking down, saw, beside the girl, a small dog seated on the other side of the fence, rapidly thumping the ground with a bushy tail.

"This is Buster, my dog," Amy continued. "I live in the house just over there." She pointed to the white painted house almost next door but separated from Uncle Jim and Aunt Dorothy's house by a vacant lot.

"I'm Tommy. I am going to spend the summer here," he replied.

Dusk had settled when the lights of the next town came into view. A motel near the roadside flaunted its flashing vacancy sign. Thomas pulled into the driveway and entered the office to arrange for a room. He would reach his destination tomorrow afternoon. Tonight he would rest. Time was catching up to him and he couldn't handle the night drives like he could all those years ago.

SHADOWS IN THE WIND

Marvin Daniels stood just outside the door of the truck stop. Sporting a cowboy hat on his head and tooled leather cowboy boots on his feet, he carried a worried expression upon his face. He inhaled deeply as he finished his cigarette, then cast a glance at the beginning of the city lights about a half mile behind the truck stop. He wondered if he shouldn't have done things a little differently. Sleeping should have been on his agenda these past few hours instead of playing the tourist.

He had been sent here by his boss, the owner of the trucking company for which he worked, to pick up an almost-new highway tractor from a local dealer and then drive it back to company headquarters at Newton, Saskatchewan, about fifty miles north of Danville Junction. He had wasted the day seeing the sights, as he had never visited this area of the U.S.A. before. Planning to leave for home the next morning, he had spent an hour at one of the local watering holes, although the tally would show he'd had only two drinks. The ringing of his cell phone an hour earlier had changed his plans. His wife, Norma, had called from their home in central Saskatchewan. She had anxiously informed him that their son, Tyler, had been hurt in a schoolyard accident and would require surgery the next day. He must return as quickly as he could.

Taking a last drag on the cigarette, he flicked the butt into the gutter and walked toward the idling tractor parked by the roadside. He would be bobtailing on this trip, no trailer behind. He climbed aboard, settled into the seat and smoothly moved the great beast into the right lane of the roadway. The bark of the diesel engine could be heard as the truck fled northward toward the Canadian border, almost four hundred miles away. Marvin stifled a yawn with his left hand as the overhead streetlights of the truck stop flashed by and the big black behemoth roared into the night. A full moon hung low in the eastern sky, but Marvin hardly noticed it. He was preoccupied with other things. The journey would be long, about sixteen hours long if he had it figured right, but he knew he could do it. He was young, invincible and he would see it through.

Amelia Bishop cast a critical eye at the figure within the mirror. At fifty-nine years of age she still retained most of her blonde hair, although a few strands of gray were visible if one looked closely. Even now her figure was relatively slim. She was looking forward to Tommy's arrival tomorrow. "What will he be like?" she thought as her memory portrayed him vividly as he was fifty years before. Mixed emotions flooded her mind as she stood there. She knew that sleep would be elusive on this night.

She turned out the light, walked over to the window of the bedroom and peered out into the moonlit night at the darkened house next door. She pictured it as it had been so long ago when Jim and Dorothy Shultz had lived there. It had been occupied by others since their time, but the population of the town had dwindled in the last few years, and the house had stood vacant for some time, peopled only by the memories of a time long gone. She stayed motionless at the window for a couple of minutes, mesmerized by the scene before her, a never-ending flatland bathed in the quicksilver light of a just risen full moon, shadowed places scattered about. The shadows held no secrets from her. In her mind she saw this land as it had appeared in the brilliant sunshine of a summer's day fifty years ago.

Thomas removed the whiskey bottle from his suitcase. He walked over to the table, which was situated in the kitchenette area of the motel room, reached for a glass, eyed it critically for a moment and poured a drink for himself. He always packed a bottle in his suitcase when he journeyed, even though he was not a heavy drinker. He found that he could relax more easily by taking a drink or two before bedtime when he traveled. He had taken his supper in the nearby café, and now he would take his ease before he sought the oblivion of sleep. The tension acquired by the day's driving seemed to flow from his being, and rest would come eventually, although for now he would reminisce a bit.

With drink in hand, he reclined upon his bed. The television was off. Never in his travels did he make use of this device as he considered the programs it broadcast an insult to human intelligence. Especially on this night, he did not need the artificial stimulation of the boob tube to aid his thinking. Taking a sip of the amber liquid, he swirled it in his mouth before swallowing, then followed his memories down that distant, winding pathway to another time, a time when the word "television" was only a wishful thought.

The closing of the screen door behind him interrupted Tommy's train of thought as Aunt Dorothy came into the front yard.

"Tommy, I would like you to run an errand for me," she began, pausing when she noticed Amy on the other side of the fence. "Oh, I see that you have met Amelia. That's good. I would like you to go to the corner store to get a loaf of bread for me. The store is three blocks from here. Maybe Amelia can show you how to get there." Handing Tommy a dollar bill, she continued, "You can each have an ice-cream cone from the change."

No further persuasion was needed. Tommy pocketed the dollar bill and looked to Amy to point the way. They started down the street with Buster in the lead looking as if it was he who would guide the group.

Tommy's gaze wandered as they made their way to the small store that was some distance away. The morning train was just now pulling into town from the west. The hissing of steam and the application of metal to metal as the brake shoes closed on steel wheels diverted Tommy's attention for a few minutes as he watched the freight train move slowly by. The sun was well up into the cloudless sky that promised a beautiful summer's day. A fragrant prairie breeze lazily carried away the smoke of the engine. An overnight shower had left the land smelling fresh and clean. Not too many people were yet about, and those who were seemed totally preoccupied with their business at hand. Buster pranced proudly ahead, finally coming to the doorway of the store, a long, low building, unpainted for many years, with a false front and the legend Lee Chan's Grocery *above the door. The dog then settled down upon the sidewalk, head resting on forepaws. Here he would wait while they conducted the business they had come for.*

Tommy and Amy entered the store and made their way to the counter. An elderly Chinese gentleman, who Tommy correctly assumed was Mr. Chan, was serving another customer, and they, in turn, waited until that transaction was complete.

"Ah, Miss Amy," began Mr. Chan, "and who is this young man with you?"

"This is Tommy, my friend," replied Amy. "He will be visiting for the summer."

Tommy shook the proffered hand and placed his order for the bread and the ice-cream cones. After receiving his fifty cents in change and his merchandise, he handed one of the cones to Amy, then thanked Mr. Chan. He and Amy turned to leave.

"One moment," began Mr. Chan. "Here is something for you." He held out two packages of bubble gum, the type with the hockey cards inside.

Once more Tommy thanked Mr. Chan as he took the gum. Passing one of the packages to Amy, he pocketed the other. They left the store to the eager welcome of Buster, who thumped the sidewalk with his tail just outside the door and eyed the ice-cream cones, clearly looking for his share. Slowly, while they enjoyed the wonderful taste of their strawberry ice-cream cones, with Buster bounding about their feet demanding their attention, they made their way back to Aunt Dorothy's house. Tommy saved the last bit of his cone and offered it to Buster, who accepted it eagerly without a moment's reservation.

Thomas smiled as he recalled those hockey cards. The gum was what he was mostly interested in at the time. The cards would usually wind up in the garbage. How ironic it seemed when he realized just what the value of those cards would be today. Truer words had never been spoken than that old saying "One man's garbage is another man's gold."

Many of the other events of that long-ago summer passed through his consciousness, a new event for almost every day. There were fishing trips to a nearby lake with Uncle Jim, even two or three occasions when Aunt Dorothy and Amy, with her parents, Joe and Mavis Stiles, accompanied them. At these times there would always be a large picnic lunch packed by Aunt Dorothy and Mrs. Stiles. Tommy and Amy would be impatient to depart early, but as these excursions were usually on a Sunday, there was always the matter of attending church service first. Other memories came to the fore, the once-weekly movie at the local theater; an occasional visit to an ice-cream parlor; the special occasion of Amy's birthday, where Tommy made many new friends; and sometimes the quiet times, just sitting on the back porch in the evening as the dusk was falling or in the afternoon of the day when the thunderheads were gathering, the rain falling in great, gushing sheets and the lightning dancing with abandon across the sky. Always there was the ever-present prairie wind. Although it could at times become almost violent, it would usually retain a

A Summer Wind

mood somewhat lesser, playful, guaranteed to blow all your cares away.

Thomas shivered inwardly as the wail of an errant night wind sounded from outside his motel room. It took him back to those childhood years when he would lie in the darkness of his room, listening to that lonesome sound but finding comfort in the fact that he was not alone, that his mother and father lay asleep in the next room. Usually the wind was a harbinger of a coming storm, but the sky had been clear when he entered his motel room. The wail of the wind sounded again as it played around the eaves of the motel, but as he listened for a repeat performance it came no more. Perhaps it had only been a messenger from somewhere in that great beyond, bearing the message that winter was not far away. It was a lost and lonesome wind, so unlike that summer wind of his youth.

"Tommy, what are you going to be when you grow up?" asked Amy as they sat side by side on the back porch.

Tommy did not reply for a few moments. He felt the passage of the night breeze through his hair as he gazed across the distant fields bathed in the silver light of the full moon. In the distance he saw the headlamp of an eastbound train, shining but dwarfed still by the separation of the miles. He pondered for a moment longer, then replied softly, "I'm going to be a railroad engineer."

They sat in silence for some minutes before Amy spoke. "I'm going to be a nurse. I will work in a big hospital and help people when they are sick."

No further conversation was necessary as they sat there in that serious moment and watched the oncoming headlight of the locomotive grow in size.

Marvin Daniels was only vaguely aware of the dull roar of the diesel engine as the moonlit miles swiftly passed. He was still preoccupied with concerns about his son's condition. While Norma had assured him that Tyler's accident was a compound fracture of the right leg, which could be surgically repaired, he knew that the ordeal would not be pleasant for his son. The glare of the headlights of oncoming vehicles was hypnotic. Again he stifled a yawn with his hand as he drove. He would stop for a coffee break at the next diner that was still open at this time of night.

Thomas reached over to pick up his wristwatch from the bedside table. It read 11:30 pm. Sleep was a long time coming tonight, even after the soothing influence of his second drink. He felt fine, the best he had been in some time, but his head would not relinquish those memories of times long gone, pleasant memories that marched through his thoughts like soldiers on parade, memories of places he had seen but mostly of the people he had known and, sadly, left behind. That summer of 1954 returned more vividly than ever before. Could he reconnect to a time that had once been? How pleasant had been those weeks of carefree camaraderie, with each new day bringing a brand-new adventure.

July had passed swiftly. August 1, 1954, was at hand. Today Uncle Jim would be busy at his workplace while Aunt Dorothy would be busy making dill pickles. The morning fled as Tommy helped with the picking and the washing of the cucumbers and the long, slender stalks of dill weed. The afternoon would be his to while away as he saw fit. He donned his cap as a protection against the hot summer sun and made his way into the back yard. Looking across the vacant lot into the Stiles' yard, he spied Amy sitting on the step, listlessly tossing a stick for Buster to fetch. The dog seemed to suffer no lack of energy as he bounded about. Tommy waved to Amy and motioned for her to join him in the field beyond the back yard. She quickly arose and scampered out the gate.

The trio, including Buster, made their way to a low rise of land some distance behind the houses and only a short distance from the railway track. Amy had earlier told Tommy that this rise of land was home to a colony of gophers, and today they would attempt to flush some of these out of their burrows by the simple practice of pouring water down the entrance holes. Tommy and Amy had earlier snuck four old buckets from Uncle Jim's storage shed. These they had secreted in a willow clump near the gopher colony. A pond was near at hand. Buster dashed about, trying in vain to catch one of the small rodents. Very quickly they all disappeared.

Tommy and Amy filled the four buckets and set them by one of the burrows. Buster sniffed about anxiously, eager to get on with the game. Quickly pouring the contents of the buckets down the entrance to the burrow, the two children scanned the area to see where a gopher would pop up. Suddenly a small head poked out of a burrow about thirty feet away. Immediately Buster gave chase, shrilly yelping in a fever of excitement. He was too late, however, and the gopher bounded into another entrance hole.

The game continued for a couple of hours, and although Buster gave his all, he had not managed to latch onto a single gopher. A steam whistle sounded as the afternoon westbound train left the station and the chuff, chuff of the engine began to pick up speed as it moved toward them. One more try was in order. Splash went the water into the burrow, and shortly a gopher dashed out of an exit near the end of the colony, only sixty or seventy feet from the railroad track. Buster led off on a merry chase. The gopher ran toward the track and the dog showed no signs of letting him get away. Tommy realized the danger and ran with all his might to head him off. The scream of the whistle and the sound of brakes echoed in Tommy's ears. He heard Amy's scream as well. The engineer had seen the danger and was trying, without any hope of success, to halt the train. The gopher shot across the track just yards ahead of the engine with Buster close behind. Tommy made a dive and managed to grab Buster's hind leg. Buster's nose hit the earth about five feet from the spinning wheels of the steam locomotive. He whirled his head about in a quick attempt to bite the hand that held him, but he finally seemed to realize just what was going on. He gave Tommy's hand a lick instead.

The slowing of the train prompted Tommy to act. He scooped Buster into his arms, and he and Amy dashed off toward the willow thickets several hundred feet away. Crouching in the sanctuary of the willows, they peered out. The train had come to a stop and the brakeman was quickly running back to the place where they had been. Looking carefully around, he removed his cap and stood for a few moments, apparently deep in thought. He scratched his head, then replaced the cap upon it, threw up his arms and walked back toward the engine. With a last call of the whistle the train began to move once more.

Amy opened her eyes with a start, having awakened from a fitful slumber. She had been dreaming. In her dreams she had been a child again with no worries or cares for tomorrow, only the sunshine of the prairie summer to fill her days. Strange, she thought, how eagerly she looked forward to Tommy's visit on the coming day. They had only known each other for a few weeks when they were children, yet the prospect of seeing him again filled her with a sense of excitement she had not felt in some time. She did not fool herself. He would, no doubt, be greatly changed by the passage of the years. A flash of memory glowed within her mind, a random vignette of a childhood on the prairie in a time that had passed so long ago.

A Summer Wind

Amy waited somewhat impatiently for Tommy's knock on the door. She always looked forward to Saturday afternoon. They would walk together to the Bijou Theater to see the matinee. Tommy loved western movies and today the picture was High Noon. The theater was about seven blocks away and they would have to leave early enough to arrive there in time for the cartoons. Presently the knock came at the front door and she hurried to open it. Her mother, at that moment, had just entered the room from the kitchen.

"Hello, Mrs. Stiles. Hi, Amy," Tommy said as he stood in the doorway, awkwardly turning his cap in his hands.

Mrs. Stiles replied, "Amy is ready to go to the show, but make sure you come home right after the picture."

"We will," replied Tommy and they quickly hurried out the door.

The two children walked briskly, not wanting to miss even the newsreel at the beginning of the picture. Amy glanced at Tommy as they moved along. Buster could not accompany them as he was not allowed in the theater. He had been left behind in the living room, refusing even to acknowledge their presence when they had prepared to leave. He had, no doubt, felt insulted that he could not come.

As Amy and Tommy passed by an alley about halfway to their destination, a large dog darted out of the alley, barking furiously. Amy was startled. She stumbled sideways and grabbed Tommy's hand to steady her balance. Tommy, not wanting to admit that he had also been momentarily frightened by the appearance of the animal, shooed the dog away in an overly loud voice. Hand in hand they walked on to the theater.

The staccato bark of the engine brake echoed across the still-darkened landscape as Marvin began his descent into the shallow valley ahead. At the bottom of the depression he spied the garish lights of a truck stop. He had crossed the border a short time before, and he had to admit to himself that he was tired. Perhaps a good breakfast with plenty of coffee would perk him up. He glanced toward the eastern horizon as he pulled into the parking lot. In a short time the sun would be up. He had no doubt that daylight would raise his spirits immensely.

The full moon was now low in the western sky, illuminating, with the aid of the pale fire of a million stars, the crossroads below. The glow of streetlights was visible in the nearby town. Traffic was almost nonexistent this early in the morning. A pair of early risers made their way toward the crossroads, one vehicle moving east to west and the other south to north. The faint *thrmmm* of the rumble strips built into the pavement could be heard as the northbound car approached the stop sign. The flash of brake lights appeared as that driver slowed to allow the westbound vehicle to continue by. When they had passed, all became still once more. A soft southern breeze tumbled a ghostly scrap of paper along the roadside. For yet another night of summer's end there was no frost. Soon the autumn nights would come with their icy winds, but for now all was hushed. This crossroad was just a quiet place in a quiet moment, a place where the river of time flowed slowly by and nothing extraordinary ever happened.

The sun was not yet up when Thomas rose from his bed. A routine that had been ingrained in him through the years would seldom allow the sun to precede his morning ritual. A quick glance out the window at the brightening sky told him that it would be warm today, no clouds in sight. His mood was upbeat. He knew that the day would be wonderful.

For the first time in recent memory Thomas cast a critical eye at the face that peered back at him from the bathroom mirror.

A Summer Wind

The lines in the face bespoke the years, years that had perhaps not been hard in ways experienced by many others, but years that had been wearing. The features suggested the durability of stone that had been sculpted and worn away by the passage of time. The hair was still largely there in quantity, but the silver threads had won a decided majority over the dark brown of memory. A slight stoop in the back and shoulders was a souvenir of that long-ago injury he had incurred in the logging industry. Splashing some aftershave lotion on his face, he exited the bathroom and began to pack his bag. His destination was still hours away and he found himself impatient to be on the road.

Marvin Daniels fought to focus his attention on the road ahead of him. He thought back to the call he had received on his cell phone while he was eating his breakfast earlier at the truck stop. His wife had anxiously informed Marvin that their son had suffered some complications from his injury, a broken blood vessel within the leg itself. He had gone into emergency surgery and she would keep him posted as things evolved. The speed of the truck fluctuated slightly, largely unnoticed by him as he forged grimly ahead. He knew in the back of his mind that he should pull over and grab a couple of hours of sleep, but home and hearth were just a few hours ahead. The brightening landscape outside his windows did not attract his attention as the never-ending monotony of the centerline went rolling by in a hypnotic cadence.

Amelia sat on the well-worn patio chair, silently absorbing the mood of the early morning as the brilliance of the sun made its presence known upon the quiet land. She didn't usually sit outside this early, but somehow she felt that this day would be special.

The cold winds of autumn would soon be at hand and she found it rather pleasant just to sit and dream for a little while in the stillness of the morning. Only the occasional sound of a car engine could be heard on the distant highway. The view before her eyes stretched to the far horizon, brown and straw-yellow stubble fields interspersed with golden poplar thickets, black patches of fallowed lands and the green of the trees that had not yet donned their fall colors. From far away came the call of a train whistle, a modern diesel locomotive signaling for a highway crossing, a harsh, abrupt sound, so unlike the heart-wrenching melody of a steam whistle heard down those corridors of memory.

Thomas scanned the far horizon. A lone sentinel of a distant grain elevator stood against the skyline, testimony to the presence of some small prairie town whose name he could not remember. It stirred the ashes of faint, long-forgotten pictures in the back of his mind; pictures that he had thought burned so long ago, memories of the ever-changing path of life on those roads of yesteryear.

The spring of 1955 had arrived at last. Tommy was eagerly looking forward to the summer holidays, when he could once again spend some time with Aunt Dorothy and Uncle Jim, although he knew that this summer's holiday would only be two or three weeks, not two months as it had been last year. His help was needed at home. Especially, although he would never admit it, he looked forward to seeing Amy once more.

The end of April was at hand. Tommy had returned home from school on a day when the promise of summer was in the air. The sun was in descent in a sky of brilliant blue, dotted here and there with fluffy white clouds hurrying across the endless expanse as though they were on their way to some important rendezvous. Tommy had just entered the kitchen when he noticed the grave expression on his mother's face.

"Tommy," she began, "I'm afraid I have some news that you will not like. We got a letter from Aunt Dorothy in the mail today. The grain company that Uncle Jim works for has transferred him to another town. It is some distance away. I know how much you were looking forward to your summer's visit, but I am afraid that will have to wait. They will be moving in about six weeks."

Crestfallen, Tommy spent the rest of the afternoon engrossed in his chores, trying not to think of how things had changed, how that unexpected circumstance had caught him unaware. Somehow the day had lost its shine, and grayness settled upon his soul.

Thomas made a slight adjustment to the wheel to allow the car to negotiate the curve in the road. Such was the road he had followed. A single curve in that distant road of life had led in a different direction entirely. Parents and other close relatives had passed on in the intervening years, and he had only traveled through Danville Junction a couple of times in later years, although the people who had been important in his life were no longer there. Once again his train of thought returned to that summer of 1954.

August 31, 1954. He couldn't believe that the summer was almost over. Tommy looked out the window of the passenger car as he waited for the lurch of the train to indicate that they were underway. The time had come for him to return home. On the station platform stood Aunt Dorothy, Uncle Jim, Mr. and Mrs. Stiles and Amy, who stood off to one side. Tommy could see the tears trickling down her cheeks as she turned her face toward him and waved goodbye. He raised his hand in farewell, trying to keep a smile on his face, but the lump in his throat would not go away. He felt the train begin to move. Slowly the station and the people standing on the platform began to grow smaller, eventually disappearing into the vast expanse of the prairie landscape. The clickety-clack of the hurrying wheels on the rail joints barely registered in his mind as the lonely call of the train whistle echoed across the countryside, adding a sense of poignancy to the moment. Tommy glanced quickly about and unobtrusively wiped a hand across his eyes. He was going home now, but somehow he felt as though a part of him had been left behind.

Amelia was in a restless mood. She had exited her door and now stood upon the back step, looking across the yard and the sun-drenched vista beyond. The red leaves of the maple tree in her back yard caught her attention. Her gaze traveled to the markings on the tree trunk about five feet from the ground. They appeared to be old letters carved into the bark. She could not make them out from where she stood, but she did not need to; she knew what they said. Her father had carved those letters so many years before. They said simply BUSTER, 1958. It was at the base of this tree that she had buried her dog, seemingly in another lifetime. A fleeting recollection of the screech of car brakes and a single yelp darted through her mind. She recalled how she had cried. Even after all these years she still felt a catch in her throat when she remembered.

The sound of a car horn jarred Marvin Daniels to attention. He swerved the big rig back to the right side of the road. This would never do. He realized that he had been a foot across the line. The hours were dragging by and he would soon be at Danville Junction. He remembered a pullout area along the road about two miles past the junction. He would have to stop and rest his weary body for a bit. He stifled a yawn with his left hand while the truck roared onward, toward the cloudless blue of the northern sky.

Marvin felt the vibration of the cell phone in his breast pock-

A SUMMER WIND

et. Expecting the worst, he flipped open the phone and tentatively said, "Hello."

He realized that the caller was his wife. She quickly told him that the surgery had been a success and their son was resting comfortably. The relief in her voice was enough to convince him that the situation was improving.

Marvin felt as though a great weight had been lifted from his shoulders. He would now definitely stop for a well-deserved nap at that pullout ahead. Somehow the sun seemed brighter now. He rolled the driver's side window down and felt the breeze blowing through his hair. The weather had stayed warm, promising to be even warmer later in the day. He felt more alive now than he had for many hours. A quick check of the highway before and behind him showed Marvin that for the moment he rode alone. With impatience clearly showing on his features, he put the hammer down.

Random memories had passed through Thomas's mind as he continued on his way. He realized suddenly that the old saying was true, driving was a no-brainer. The car navigated well even when his thoughts were many decades away. He was only a couple of miles from the crossroads near Danville Junction. He felt the spur of impatience and accelerated somewhat. He would soon be there. The land here was very flat, and the bush had been gone for as long as he could remember. Far away, somewhat to his right, he could see a highway tractor moving toward the crossroad. He took no notice of it. The highway tractor was in another place, another time. It had no bearing whatever on his existence.

Marvin Daniels abruptly corrected his line of travel as he realized

33

SHADOWS IN THE WIND

that his eyes had closed once again. The brief burst of euphoria that he had experienced after the telephone call from his wife had worn off and he knew that the time had come to stop and rest. The junction was just ahead. Only two more miles remained to the pullout beyond. Concentration, that was the key, eyes open, senses alert. The hot wind fanned his face while the September scent teased his mind, invoking pleasant thoughts of other times, other times with no stress, no worries. Eyes open, senses alert. How pleasant it would be to relax in his recliner at home. The reclining chair had a built in-vibrator. He could almost feel the *thrmmm* of the vibrator as he lay back. It would be so wonderful but not now. Eyes open, senses alert. Only two more miles.

Thomas realized that the junction was just ahead. To his right he noticed, absently, the approach of the highway tractor. Thomas knew he had the right-of-way and did not give it a second thought. Danville Junction was in his sight. He wondered what would lie at the end of this road. The junction was only a hundred and fifty feet away. Suddenly he realized that the large tractor bearing down on the intersection had not slackened its speed. He was seized by a moment of indecision just before he applied extreme braking. The black hood of the highway tractor loomed to his right. Thomas's hand automatically depressed the horn. Memory raced through his mind and he could see it all again, a kaleidoscope of color, then oblivion.

Impatience dogged Amelia's thoughts. She made a cup of tea and took it out to the patio table where she now sat. Time, on this day, seemed forever. Forever, she suddenly realized, could also apply to the scene before her eyes, the checkered farmland stretching to

A Summer Wind

the far horizon, seeming to lie dormant in the heat of the golden sun and the warmth of the memories locked forever within her mind. It was a land reaching toward eternity, having changed little over the fleeting years. A picture of Tommy, as he had been fifty years before, passed through her thoughts. Surely he could not be far away now.

Amelia took a sip of her tea as she gazed across the near distance at the area between the back fence and the railroad track. She gazed into the heat that lay upon the land like a blanket, making everything near the surface appear indistinct, even blurry. For a moment or two she could swear that she saw two figures emerging from the shimmering heat waves. They appeared to be a boy and a dog. Slowly they seemed to materialize some distance before her. She strained to discern their identity, but just as quickly as they appeared they melted away. Nothing remained but the undulations of the air mass in the heat of the day.

The honking of a horn snapped Marvin's thoughts to full alert. The crossroad, with a car immediately to his left, leapt into view. Before he could take any action, the crossroad had passed behind and a quick glance in his rearview mirror told him that the other vehicle was okay. "No point in stopping now," he thought. Shivers ran down his back as he realized what a near miss it had been. It was time for rest, less than a mile away now. He wondered if he would be able to close his eyes.

Thomas could not believe his eyes. His car was stopped in the middle of the crossroad. The truck had passed, but Thomas knew without a doubt that not a hand's width had separated the front of his car from the rear wheels of the truck. Slowly he moved his car

SHADOWS IN THE WIND

ahead, parked on the shoulder and lay his arms and head on the steering wheel. After gathering his wits a bit, Thomas straightened up and glanced over his left shoulder before easing the car back onto the roadway. As he began to drive that last, short distance to Danville Junction, he appreciated what a wonderful day it really was.

The crossroads lay silent in the sweltering heat of the day, as though exhausted from some gargantuan effort. No traffic was in sight in any direction. A slight breeze had sprung up and a dust devil meandered across an adjacent field, making its lonely way to wherever dust devils go. It was a quiet moment, in a quiet place, where the river of time flowed slowly by and nothing significant ever happened. A single red maple leaf fluttered across the roadway, looking like a gaily colored butterfly on a road to nowhere, carried along on a summer wind.

HOTEL

It wasn't much of a hotel, as hotels go — just a weather-beaten clapboard structure of indeterminate age, two-and-a-half stories in height with dormer windows set into the roofline of ancient cedar shingles. It appeared to be abandoned except for the single illuminated sign above the door that said *Beer Parlor*, barely decipherable in the early shadow of dusk. Parked in front were two aging pickup trucks indicating that perhaps there were some customers inside. Across the street sat an old grain elevator, towering above the hotel, not with a stately grace but rather with the tired air of something that has outlived its usefulness. A closer inspection revealed that it had been a long time since the access road had felt the touch of the wheels of commerce, and, indeed, the railroad grade that ran beside the elevator was devoid of rails. Only bats inhabited the ancient structure, bats and old dreams.

Charlie took in this scene, surveying the scattered cluster of houses that made up the town. The main street, where his car was now parked, was of gravel, and a faint tinge of dust still hung in the evening air. He did not know the name of this town. If there had been a sign posted somewhere on the outskirts, he had somehow missed it. He had taken this obscure side road off the main highway with no thought except to see where it led. Here, situated in the vast expanse of the undulating prairie, some thirty kilometers from the main highway, was the reason for the road's existence. Perhaps this sleepy little town would suit his purpose and yield to him that which he sought.

Charlie was a writer, or at least he thought that he was. For

SHADOWS IN THE WIND

some time he'd had an idea that there were stories hidden here in the vast prairie, stories carried in the minds of its inhabitants. He would attempt to unlock some of these stories. No doubt these country hicks would be easy pickings for a suave, sophisticated man of the world like himself. What better place to approach people than a little country pub. As he thought about his plans, he decided that he should see if the establishment still rented rooms, as he would need facilities for the coming night.

Opening the door, Charlie stepped into the softly lit interior. He saw that the sign outside had erred just a little. The beer parlor was actually through a second, closed door to his left. To his right was what appeared to be a dining room, empty now, with a vintage grandfather clock in one corner. Directly ahead was a counter. No one was present there, but a small silver bell reposed upon its surface. Charlie looked pensively at it for one moment, then picked it up and rang it twice. In a matter of seconds the door to his left opened and a middle-aged, balding man stepped through, giving Charlie an inquisitive glance as he approached.

"Yes, sir, what can I do for you?" queried the man, whom Charlie assumed was the proprietor.

"I need a room for a couple of nights. I wonder if you have one available for rent?" Charlie answered.

"Well now," came the answer, "it's been some time since we've had anyone stay over, but I think that we can accommodate you. I have a couple of rooms that are available just off the beer parlor. Nothing fancy but they're clean. By the way, I'm Jack," he added as he extended his hand in a gesture of welcome.

Charlie thanked the innkeeper, signed the register, paid the agreed-upon price in advance, retrieved his bag from the car and followed the man through a doorway just behind the counter, finding himself in a hallway leading off to the left. He saw a flight of stairs at the far end leading to the upper stories of the building.

HOTEL

Off to his left was a closed door that he assumed led back to the beer parlor. To his right were two more doors along the expanse of the hall. The innkeeper stopped beside the first one and, turning, saw Charlie looking at the stairway.

"The upper floors are closed up now. Haven't been near enough customers to warrant the expense of maintenance, although that wasn't always the case. I remember Granddad telling my father that back in the twenties the place was sold out every weekend. I'll put you in this room here. If you want any supper you can eat in the dining room. We have a very limited menu, but my wife will fix you something. After the bar closes there will be no one on the premises, so I will leave you a key to the exit door at the near end of this hallway. The rest of the building will be locked up."

Thanking his host once again, Charlie stepped into his room. Looking it over he saw that it was, as promised, clean but furnished in a manner somewhat similar to the house of his grandparents, remembered from so many years ago. He deposited his bag on the single chair, availed himself of the ancient washroom to remove the grime accumulated in a day's travel and made his way to the dining room.

Sitting at his table in the dining room, Charlie wondered at the hush of the place, broken only by the monotonous tick-tock of the ancient grandfather clock off in the corner. A cold chill passed through him, completely inconsistent with the temperature outside. He had ordered his meager supper of pizza and a side salad, and Jack, the proprietor, had taken his order and left, leaving him to look around the room with a sense of unease. His meal arrived and he ate hurriedly. After downing the last cup of coffee he pushed his plate away, paid his bill and made his way to the bar where his real quest would begin.

The first thing Charlie noticed upon entering the beer parlor

SHADOWS IN THE WIND

was that there were only two patrons present, probably the owners of the vintage pickup trucks he had earlier seen parked outside. He studied them for a moment. Both appeared to be in their seventies, although the similarity ended there. One was a large individual with a full head of silver gray hair and a drooping paunch, while the other was a smaller man, slight of build, with a receding hairline. Both had a leathery appearance, as though they spent a great deal of time outdoors. Charlie shrugged; these would be very likely candidates to woo in his search for a story. He walked up to their table.

"Evening, gents," Charlie said as he approached. "I was wondering if I could join you fellows. I'd be pleased to buy you a drink."

The larger of the individuals looked up pensively for a moment. "Sure, stranger, come and set. I'm Mark Wilkes. My buddy there is Harold Johnson. Anyone who offers to buy is certainly welcome."

"Charlie Samuels here," returned Charlie, shaking hands all around and pulling back a chair. He ordered drinks and the trio continued with the preliminaries.

"Harold and I are ranchers, although now largely retired. My place is only a couple of kilometers out of town. Harold's is more like twenty," continued Mark.

Charlie responded, "I'm a writer by trade. I've always been of the opinion that there are hidden stories out in these rural areas, stories that would be highly interesting to the reading public. I'm going to spend a couple of days in town to sort of see what turns up."

Harold looked at Mark thoughtfully. "Mark, do you think we should tell him about the killing?"

Glancing back at his friend, almost disapprovingly, Mark replied, "I dunno Harold, that's mighty old news, must be sev-

HOTEL

enty-eight or seventy-nine years ago."

By now Charlie was intrigued. "Give me the story. I'm certain it will be interesting."

Hesitantly, Mark began. "Well, as you might suspect, neither Harold nor myself can give you a firsthand account as it was before our time. I'm seventy-seven years old. Harold is only seventy. I first heard about it from the local gossip when I was but a lad. You have to understand that, at the time, this place was booming. The railroad had arrived only a few years previously. My dad had settled here some twenty years before. Harold's father was a relative newcomer then. It was only about two years since his arrival. Strangers were a common sight in town. The hotel was usually full. At that time the second floor was open and there were also a couple of rooms put into the loft area of the third floor."

Mark paused for a sip of his beer, staring unseeingly at the glass as his mind wandered the back roads of his memory. "As I recall, there was this fellow come into town. Johnny is the name that comes to mind. He was probably in his thirties and he took a room in the loft, paying by the week. What his business was I don't remember, but he kept pretty much to himself. A couple of weeks later a traveling salesman arrived in town. Funny, but I can't put a name to him after all these years. Anyway, as the story goes, he also took a room in the hotel. One Saturday night he and Johnny got into an awful fight. Johnny fell and hit his head. When he came to, he staggered off to his room. No one laid eyes on him for a couple of days, everyone thinking he was sulking in his room. Well, about the third morning the salesman turned up with his throat cut, blood everywhere; no sign of a weapon. The police arrived and conducted a thorough investigation."

"How awful," interrupted Charlie. "Where did this occur?"

"Why, right here in this hotel, in the dining room."

Charlie felt a shiver run down his spine as he remembered

41

SHADOWS IN THE WIND

the chill he had earlier felt while sitting at the supper table.

Mark continued with the story. "The police did a room-by-room check of the premises. When they arrived at Johnny's room, they could raise no one inside. They called on the innkeeper to open the door with the master key. Inside they found Johnny, dead, with his bloodied straight razor clutched tightly in his hand. The solution to the murder, you say? When the doctor examined Johnny he swore that he had probably been dead for a couple of days, probably shortly after the fight. They never could figure the exact story behind this, so it sort of got filed under unknown, forgotten after these many years."

The mood grew somber then, and all sat quietly for a few moments in thought.

"Yes, sir," piped up Harold. "That was about the way I heard it too, although a few years later."

Charlie wondered now if it had been a wise decision to take a room in this place, but he quickly dismissed the worry. He had never believed in ghosts, and these characters were probably pulling his leg.

"Well, gents," said Harold, "you'll have to excuse me for a few minutes but I'll have to use the facilities. I think I overdid the beer tonight."

After Harold had left, Mark gazed after him for a moment. He then turned to Charlie and spoke. "You know, Harold doesn't know all the facts behind that story, and what I'm about to tell you has never been substantiated, but his father had a reputation for being a practical joker, and rumor had it that he instigated the fight between Johnny and the salesman. He told Johnny some story that caused him to accost the salesman. I don't know how credible this was, but I do know that Harold's father was dead set against practical jokers for all the years I knew him. Perhaps this episode had cured him of this disposition."

HOTEL

Harold returned to the table and they sat around making small talk for a while. The witching hour came and went. Eventually all rose to go their separate ways, and Charlie proceeded to his room, tired after his long day.

Charlie awoke with a start. Something had disturbed him, perhaps the slow beating of his own heart. No, on second thought, that wasn't his heart beating. It was the tick-tock of the grandfather clock, carrying from the dining room in the eerie stillness. He lay there listening. He was certain that some noise or other disruption from the normal had lifted him from slumber. He reached over and took his watch from the night table, depressing the light display as he checked the time, 2:30 am. All was now quiet.

He was about to turn over to try to resume his rest when he heard a distinct *thump* from the hallway outside. This was followed by a *clump, clump, clump*, like footsteps descending the staircase from the upper floors. What nonsense was this? He quickly put on his pants, shirt and shoes and eased open his hallway door, peering fretfully into the dim hallway lighting. There was nothing to be seen but the stairway at the end of the hall, which rose to the landing where the stairs reversed to continue upward, beyond his vision.

Slowly he walked to the stairwell. As he reached the end of the hall, he looked up to the top of the stairs, now visible to his gaze. There was a door at the top of these stairs. Normally he would not have expected to see one there, but, as he had earlier been informed, the upper floors had been closed for years. The door stood partly open.

Carefully he climbed the stairs. Beyond the door, all was in darkness. He turned on a switch at the head of the stairs and pale light flooded the upstairs hallway. At least the lights still worked

43

up here. He could see that this section of the hotel had indeed not been used in some time as dust was prevalent and cobwebs decorated the corners.

At the end of this hallway was a second staircase, similar to the first, leading to the upper loft. After climbing these stairs, Charlie tried a second light switch. No response. No power here. In the gloom he could make out a window at the far end of the loft. The watery moonlight filtered in, allowing him to make out two doors to his left, both closed. He paused and listened carefully.

Swish, swish, swish, swish. Charlie heard this noise distinctly. It seemed to be coming from behind the first door. Puzzled, he thought for a moment. Where had he heard that noise before? Suddenly it became crystal clear. He was transported back in time to his grandfather's house. His grandfather was sharpening his razor on a leather strop in preparation for shaving, *swish, swish, swish, swish.*

The hair on the back of Charlie's head seemed to stand straight up, and cold chills rushed down his spine. He turned and ran down the two flights of stairs to the main hallway. As he ran to his room, he glimpsed, from the corner of his eye, hidden in the half gloom, what appeared to be a head. The door to his room stood open, as he had left it. His suitcase, which he had repacked against some intuitive eventuality, stood just inside. He grabbed it and raced out the side door of the hotel, pausing only long enough to slip the lock. Quickly he started his car and raced into the night, back to the main highway and civilization, away from this insanity.

Back at the hotel the silence was broken by the creaking of the door that led from the bar to the hallway. Mark and Harold stepped through, Harold chuckling softly. "We sure threw a scare into that city slicker. I thought he would burn up the rug with his speed. I never did fancy them city folk. I've always thought they looked down their noses at us. It's a good thing we know where Jack hides his keys."

Mark looked somber. "I don't think we should have done this Harold. I'm not proud of this night's work." He reached down and picked up the baseball that Harold had thrown against the wall on the stairwell, causing it to roll down the stairs sounding ever so much like footsteps.

Harold was still chuckling. "I wonder, though, why he went upstairs? I thought that Jack kept that door locked for years."

"I don't know and I don't care. I'm heading for home. Are you leaving too?"

"No," came the answer, "I've had too much beer tonight. I don't fancy that long drive. Here's a room going begging, already paid for. I think I'll grab a three-hour snooze. I've never stayed in this hotel before, and Jack doesn't get here before eight. I'll be gone by then."

"Suit yourself. I'll see you tomorrow." Mark turned and walked out the door, closing it behind him.

Harold stretched out on the bed, luxuriating in its comfort. After a couple of minutes he drifted off to sleep. Had he been listening outside that loft room, two floors above, he would have heard *swish, swish, swish, swish*. Abruptly the sound ceased. A moment later the door began to open.

MARTY

Carefully pouring a cup of cold coffee from the morning pot, George placed it in the microwave oven and heated it on the high setting for one minute. He then added a dash of low-fat milk and placed the cup on the table beside his favorite armchair. He lowered himself into the chair somewhat stiffly, reflecting his seventy-four years of age, then settled back and opened the newspaper that he had bought at the corner store scarcely half an hour earlier. The *Winnipeg Free Press*. He hadn't seen one of these in years. A wave of nostalgia had washed over him the instant he laid eyes on it in the news rack. Living in Vancouver these past fifty-six years had left him slightly out of touch with the prairie, but the paper had caught his eye and on a whim he had bought a copy. Relaxing, he began to scan the pages.

Little of the information contained in the newspaper differed from what would be offered in the Vancouver *Province* or *Sun*, and as George read on he sometimes forgot the distant origin of this missive. When he remembered, he wondered if he might have wasted his money on this purchase.

The obituary page finally came to his attention. Casually glancing at the names listed, one in particular leapt out at him. *Martin Searles*. This name certainly struck a chord. Martin, also seventy-four years of age, had left this mortal coil on August 29. The column gave a summary of Martin's life: growing up on the prairies of Manitoba; serving in Europe in the last months of the war; being wounded and decorated; eventually returning to Winnipeg to pursue a career in small business, and retiring in 1984.

Reading through the obituary, George's thoughts drifted back more than half a century to the time when he had last seen Martin — about 1944 if memory served him correctly. He recalled that they had both tried to enlist in the army, eager to join their countrymen in Europe. Martin was accepted while George was rejected for medical reasons, flat feet to be exact. George's last memory of him was when Martin had waved goodbye as the train pulled out of the station at Ochre River, carrying him to Winnipeg.

Glancing out the living room window at the golden, mid-afternoon sunshine of early September, George allowed his mind to wander down the corridor of time to early September 1941 when he had first met Martin. George, at fifteen years of age, was bursting with enthusiasm to enlist in the service of his country, to travel the world and take part in the great adventure that was now being experienced by so many of his countrymen. Unfortunately, he had thought, another three years would have to pass before he would be of an age to go.

Odd, it seemed to George, the vividness of the memory. Growing up on a farm in the Magnet area of Manitoba, having survived the rigors of the Depression years, he found that prospects, for the population in general, improved with the advent of the war. While many of the young men had enlisted, others were employed in the war effort at home. George, at his age, was pretty much limited to the occasional employment on local farms. Crops had improved since the thirties, and farm labor was in short supply. George lived with his parents on a small farm and found that he needed the extra employment to generate some added income.

Robert Jackson, owner of one of the larger farms in the area, had his own threshing outfit and did custom work as well as his own harvesting. George had hired on for the harvest. This same crew would, perhaps, harvest seven or eight farms. Any members of the threshing crew who lived within a short distance usually

MARTY

drove their teams home at the end of the day, but others far from home were billeted at the farm where the harvest was in progress, and it was at the Jackson farm that George first met Martin. They hit it off immediately and over the next three years would become fast friends.

George was busily engaged at his noon meal. He did not participate in the conversation around the large table. He felt somewhat intimidated by the fact that the rest of the men on the threshing crew were considerably older than he was. The war effort had taken the younger men of the region, leaving only the very young and what seemed to him the very old. The next-youngest man in the crew, Albert Parr, seemed to George very ancient indeed at forty-seven years of age.

"Mister Jackson," as George in his youthful age would address the boss, was not in the room at the moment, having risen to a summons by his wife. Shortly he re-entered the dining room followed by a younger man, about George's age, fair of complexion with blond hair, a tall, lean build and a wide grin on his face.

"Men," Mr. Jackson began, "I'd like to introduce you to my nephew, Martin Searles. He hails from the Makinak district and he is joining us for the rest of the harvest season."

Martin shook hands all around. When he came to George, he smiled and said, "Marty's the name and, I guess, harvesting is the game." George took an instant liking to the newcomer, and as Marty sat down in the empty chair next to him, George found that he had someone to converse with as they fell to their interrupted meal.

George settled deeper into his comfortable chair, feeling the tide of old memories wash over him, memories that had not entered his consciousness for years, memories of sunlit days, hard but satisfying physical labor, times of youthful comradeship when the world was theirs for the taking and the clouds of uncertainty and doubt were seldom seen. He reached for his coffee cup, which sat on the table beside him. Taking a sip, he found that it had acquired a somewhat bitter taste, unlike the remembered coffee of his youth.

The rest of the threshing crew was already seated around the large table when George and Marty entered after hurriedly washing up at the washbasin on the porch. As they took their seats, Alex Smith looked up from his meal and said, "Here's George and Marty, knights of the order of the hollow leg." In two short days, George and Marty had established a reputation for prodigious appetite, and once again they fell to with a gusto that only youth can display. Mrs. Jackson, being of Ukrainian descent, set a bountiful table loaded with perogies, cabbage rolls and homemade sausage as well as chicken or pork and usually a tasty dessert. Seldom were leftovers a problem. Soon the noon hour ended and all rose to resume their labor. Time was marching on.

Putting down his coffee cup, George remembered again the time, more than a half century before, when midafternoon would herald the arrival of a lunch in the field. In early September this would often consist of tomato sandwiches and coffee: homemade bread spread with hand-churned butter, with slices of tomatoes ripened by a blazing prairie sun and watered only by the rain. Their flavor could not be described to someone who had not savored them. A piece of cake or a couple of cookies would cap this lunch, all made that morning in the farm kitchen and only a memory by nightfall. The meal would be washed down with hot coffee, made heavenly with the addition of farm-fresh cream and a generous portion of sugar, which, in retrospect, was surprising as rationing was in effect. Somehow there always

MARTY

seemed to be enough for the harvest season.

With a disdainful glance at the coffee cup beside him, George thought again of his friend. Marty had always been an exuberant type, outgoing and ready to tackle any job that came his way, seeming to fear nothing. As George discovered, though, Marty did have one flaw. He had an irrational fear of snakes. Just the sight of one would send him into a blind panic, although only momentarily. Chuckling, George remembered fondly.

The sheaves were coming thick and fast as George struggled to build his load. Marty was, as usual, bending his back with a will, exulting in the glory of youth and strength. The September sun bathed the field in a golden glow only slightly diffused by smoke from a far-off grass fire. George paused for a moment, wiping his brow and breathing deeply of the perfume of summer's end. The horse team plodded slowly along. The hayrack was about half full.

As Marty pitched a sheaf onboard, a long garter snake, black with yellow stripes, slid from the bundle and landed at Marty's feet. Immediately he threw his arms in the air and leaped backward, losing his pitchfork in the process. The pitchfork arced through the air, tumbling end over end, finally landing with tines down on the left horse's rump. The horse snorted and reared, pawing at the air and startling his teammate. Then they were off. George, unprepared for the sudden movement, was thrown head over heels off the hayrack, fortunately landing in the middle of the scattered sheaves. He picked himself off the ground after ascertaining that everything still worked and watched as the horses galloped into the distance while Marty stood sheepishly by.

With hayrack bouncing wildly and sheaves strewn along the way, the horses entered a poplar thicket. Trying to pass on opposite sides of a large poplar tree proved to be their undoing. The neck yoke hit the tree; the hayrack left the wagon and came to a stop against the horses' hindquarters, halting all progress. Eventually, as George and Marty approached, a relative calm was restored to the scene.

Mr. Jackson, who had witnessed the whole performance, was not far behind. He surveyed the scene of chaos before him. Saying not a word, merely shaking his head from side to side, he proceeded to untangle the mess.

Supper that night was an awkward time for the boys, with the others of the crew ribbing them a little. Needless to say, Marty spent the rest of the season hauling grain from the threshing machine to the grain bin some distance away. Snakes did not hide in the grain.

The staccato bark of a diesel truck as the engine brake was applied wakened George from his reverie. The presence of a major thoroughfare nearby reminded him that peace and quiet were commodities not available in this present day. Glancing out the window, he saw that the sun was far along in its journey through the western sky. Shrugging, he adjusted his position in his armchair and allowed his mind to drift again through the ages to a time when the daylight seemed to last forever, to the year of his sixteenth birthday and another August when the harvest began once more.

The work was done for the day. The threshing crew had washed up and filed into the house to begin their evening meal. Marty had stopped at the wooden outhouse to address some unfinished business. As he sat there, he looked out through a crack in the weathered boards. A machine shed was in his view. Behind the shed was an old steel-wheeled tractor. It had obviously been there for years, minus an engine and with one front wheel missing.

He was about to conclude his visit when he saw movement. On closer inspection he saw Uncle Bob making his way to the old

MARTY

tractor. Glancing about, Uncle Bob took a wrench from some hidden location and removed the gear-case cover from the machine. Reaching inside, he brought forth a bottle filled with a clear liquid. Tucking it under his arm he proceeded to the house.

Marty realized that he had just seen the location of Uncle Bob's stash of home-brewed whiskey, the making of which was highly illegal and punishable by stiff fines, thus necessitating the secrecy. A few minutes later he also entered the dining room. He took his place just as the bottle made the round, although his and George's glasses were filled to a somewhat lower level than those of the other field hands. George accepted this double standard. He realized that they were just reaching the threshold of the adult fraternity. In time he knew they would achieve their proper standing. Marty, on the other hand, slightly resented the fact that, by his way of thinking, they were not treated as equals.

Saturday evening finally arrived. The work of the harvest would not resume until Monday morning, as Uncle Bob and many of the field hands still observed Sunday as a day of rest. Marty and George had made plans to attend a dance in Magnet, at the community hall. As the town was six miles away, this would involve a brisk walk. A weekly bath was in order. This was accomplished by the use of a washtub set up in a small structure behind the machine shed.

Marty, after completing his ablutions and donning clean clothes, left George to his preparations and wandered over to the old tractor. Looking around carefully, he reached for the wrench and unfastened the lid of the gear case. Lifting out a full bottle of home-brewed whiskey, he picked up an identical empty bottle that he had earlier hidden nearby. Reaching into the rusted gear case, he broke the bottom of the bottle. No doubt Uncle Bob would think that a full bottle had accidentally been broken.

George had by this time completed his preparations, and the two set off for town.

Striding along briskly in the early dusk, the miles quickly fell behind. A gigantic golden moon hung low in the eastern sky, seeming to watch over their progress. A warm, fitful breeze blew softly from the south, and a slight hint of dust from earlier traffic still hung in the evening air. The call of a hunting owl was heard in the twilight. Visible in the night sky were the winking lights of military aircraft honing their hunting skills on the practice ranges on the shores of Lake Dauphin.

Occasionally pausing to take a sip from the bottle, Marty and George were feeling rather fine by the time they arrived at the hall. Secreting the treasured bottle in a corner of the wood-pile behind the hall, they went inside. Here again was evidence of the times as noted by the absence of younger men. The orchestra, consisting of a guitar, a fiddle, an accordion and a set of drums, was carrying on in a lively fashion, perhaps trying to drown out the fact of the war raging so far away.

George knew many of the people here as his home was only four miles to the north. Almost all were strangers to Marty, whose home was some miles away, but he quickly got into the swing of things, cutting a rug with many available partners. George, being somewhat bashful, tended to sit out many of the dances. Occasionally he would summon up the courage to escort some young lady onto the floor either at his or, more often, at her initiative. Once in a while he wandered outside to seek another drop of courage from the hidden bottle.

By the time the orchestra played the final waltz, George was beginning to feel slightly ill. He and Marty set out on the long journey home. To George it seemed as though the distance had increased tenfold. The yellow moon now hung low in the western sky. It did not seem quite as bright as it had been in early evening, and at times George could have sworn that there were, in fact, two moons in his vision.

Finally, after what seemed an eternity, they arrived at the Jackson farm just as daybreak was showing in the east. Sunday was the longest day of all.

Sitting ever so still, with a half smile on his face, George rehashed those glory days of youth when the biggest concern was whether a third helping of supper was in order. He recalled the frugal meals he had eaten since the passing of his wife some years back. He'd had to watch his diet these last years, and he often lost his desire to do the cooking, which made him appreciate these memories even more fondly. This journey into yesteryear became suffused with the color of understanding, understanding the secrets of the universe, after all these years.

One by one the years drifted by. News of the war's progression was always a main topic of conversation whenever and wherever people gathered. When 1944 arrived, George turned eighteen in July while Marty reached that plateau in early August. This was the year they would achieve their goal to live that adventure that had taken the world by storm. First there was one final harvest to complete.

The threshing crew was once more gathered around the dining room table in the Jackson household. This was the final day of the harvest season. George and Marty were in a jubilant mood. In two days they would leave for Winnipeg to enlist in the Canadian army, to enter the fray and change the course of world history. Such were the dreams, but sometimes the cold dawn of reality comes all too soon. The glasses around the table were filled once again. All were filled to the brim. The older hands drank a toast to the younger men, perhaps wishing in their own mind that they could make that journey and also do their part.

The harvest was ended and tomorrow was another day.

George stood before the examining doctor, unable to believe his ears. Surely this couldn't be true. "Rejected" was the word he heard. Rejected as unfit for service. Flat feet were the reason. Marty had been accepted while he had not. Gone were the dreams. The taste of defeat was bitter in his mouth, defeat because he had not even had the opportunity to participate, to offer his service, to turn the tide, to crush the tyrant and make the world a better place to live. Sadly this could now never be.

The cold, crisp air of an October evening sent a chill through George as he stood there watching the train. Steam issued from the engine as the throttle was advanced and the drivers began to turn. A golden prairie moon hung over the small town of Ochre River as he witnessed the departure of his friend, wishing he could be on that train as well. He lifted his hand in farewell as he saw Marty wave from the window of the passenger car. Slowly the train picked up speed, and the sound of the steam whistle echoed across the prairie as the road crossing was approached. With a heavy feeling in his heart, George slowly turned and walked away. A thought drifted through his mind, something that the examining doctor had said when he gave George the devastating news of his rejection for service. "I understand how you feel, but if you really want to serve your country, I believe that there is a shortage of workers in the shipyards at Vancouver. Their work is as important to the war effort as anybody's."

George suddenly realized that he had spent the entire afternoon sitting in his armchair reminiscing. Outside, dusk had fallen, and inside a heavy gloom had descended. He had not noticed the darkness because he knew that one does not need light to look at the pictures in the mind. He recalled the aftermath of his failure

MARTY

to enter the armed forces. In the month of November 1944, he had bid his family goodbye and made his way to Vancouver, British Columbia, where he spent the remainder of the war in the shipyards. After the war he had obtained employment as a longshoreman. Here he had worked until his retirement in 1990. He had made the journey back to his home a few times until the death of his mother some thirty-five years earlier. His father had passed on several years prior to that. He seemed to find little reason to make the trek these last years. Marty, upon his return from the war, had settled in Winnipeg, running a business that sold farm equipment of some sort. Destiny had ordained that their paths would never cross again.

George looked out the window and saw that the moon had risen, seeming somehow smaller than the prairie moons of his memories. He marveled at how quickly the years had passed, how the seasons of life had vanished and winter was at hand. He thought of a poem he had read that had been written by a forgotten poet some years previously. It was called, aptly, "Seasons."

> There's a silence in the meadow now
> near the end of the waning day.
> The mind still sometimes wonders how
> the seasons have passed away.
>
> From the spring time of a youth long past
> when the rainbows brightly shone.
> To a winter cold and gray at last,
> all the battles long since done.
>
> We have trod the fertile fields of dreams
> through the seasons set in time.
> Walked the lonesome valleys, crossed swollen streams,
> many mountains we have climbed. .

Now the days grow short past summers end
and the rose's blooms now cease.
The mighty oak trees sway and bend
'neath the rising autumn breeze.

The leaves of summer, now so bold
near the time of the day's sunset,
shining in their autumn gold
but there is some time left yet.

Life's twilight comes now oh so soon
but we know we still must try
just to live by the light of a golden moon
set into a painted sky.

"Good-bye, Marty," thought George. "May a golden prairie moon forever light your way." He closed the paper and set it on the table beside him.

YESTERDAY'S SUMMER

She would not see the winter. Somehow she had known this even before Dr. Rae had confirmed the fact. The increasing discomfort and occasional fleeting pain, coupled with the lack of appetite and gradual weight loss, had hinted very strongly that all was not well. Procrastination had always been a vice of hers, and she had delayed seeking professional evaluation for too long.

Edie stirred her tea. A relaxing cup here on the covered veranda was something she had long treasured, especially on a warm, sunny afternoon like today with the balmy spring breeze gently stirring the blooming lilac bushes in the back yard and the sight of billowy white clouds moving across the endless sky, lazily going on their journey to wherever clouds go. The croaking of the frogs from a nearby pond could be heard through the screened enclosure, and the various wildflowers dotted the meadows and fields stretching to the far horizon. Spring was in its glory here on the Saskatchewan plain.

Edie's thoughts turned inward momentarily. She recalled that she had paused in front of the mirror in the living room when she returned from the doctor's office. The face that had looked back had been almost a stranger to her and yet somehow familiar, as though she had once known her but lost touch over the years. Seventy years of age, looking wan and thin with graying brown hair, but still showing traces of the beauty that had once been hers. A smile slowly creased her face as she drifted back in time.

The year was 1952. Edie had never been so happy in her twenty years of life. This was her night, hers and Martin's. She had met

Martin just eight short months ago. He had swept her off her feet with his quick smile and vibrant personality. Martin was a local farmer, struggling, to be sure, but he let no grass grow beneath his feet. When he proposed, Edie was quick to accept, and this was the culmination of their dream, their wedding night. Although there had been no extra money for a town wedding with the lavish reception, Edie did not think that it could be any more perfect than the ceremony here, in the yard of his parents' home, in the company of friends, with a full prairie moon hanging in a star-studded sky and a sense of mystery instilled by the limitless void beyond, hinting at a future, unknown but surely filled with points of light amidst the darker moments of life.

Taking a sip from the teacup, Edie recalled those first years. Hard work had been the norm. There had been some darker moments, but the points of light had certainly been there as well. Then came that darkest moment, some thirty years ago, just one month before their twentieth anniversary. Martin had left home that morning driving the brand-new tractor that they had purchased only the week before. He had planned on doing about four hours of work in a field about half a mile away. He would be home for lunch. Noon had come and gone. He had not returned.

Edie shuddered as the painful memory surfaced. She lifted her eyes to follow the path of a single gull in a vain attempt to escape the shadows in her mind. In vain it was indeed, and the memory returned once more.

The clock on the kitchen wall read 2:30 pm. Edie anxiously watched for Martin's return, hoping that the job was taking some extra time to complete. She finally decided to investigate. Hurrying along on foot across that half-mile distance, she reached the field but the tractor was not in sight. She paused to listen. The sound of an engine running was music to her ears. It came from just

YESTERDAY'S SUMMER

behind a small copse of poplar trees near one corner of the field. She hastened toward it and almost fainted when she saw that the machine was high-centered on a boulder at the edge of the field, one rear wheel off the ground, slowly turning, ever turning. The disc was still hitched behind the tractor. Behind the disc lay Martin, crushed beyond recognition.

Wiping a tear from her eye, Edie could not remember how she had summoned the strength to run to the nearest neighbor a half mile away. She could recall only in part the following weeks, the funeral, the ensuing investigation and the crumbling of her ordered world. Nobody could ever say exactly what had happened. Nobody could ever know.

Reaching out toward the western horizon with her eyes, Edie remembered her insistence on placing the veranda to face this direction when they had built this house some thirty-five years before. She had loved this view, the limitless fields bordered by their flower carpet of spring with the occasional hedgerow of poplar or willows, filled later in the summer with the ripening grain dancing in the August breeze like waves upon the sea. She treasured the sight of the summer storms lighting the sky with all their glory, the roll of the heavenly cannons deafening. Even the winters rested gently in her memories, the curtain of drifting snow blowing across the fields, moving wraithlike across the frozen landscape illuminated only by the sepulchral light of a watery February sun. Here in her home she had felt secure, warm and loved.

Edie felt the beginning of the pain. She reached for the vial of pills on the table nearby. Swallowing the painkiller, she closed her eyes for a few minutes, allowing the numbing of the senses to begin. As she rested she thought once more of those bygone years. After Martin's death she had continued operating the mixed farm that she and Martin had built. Although this had entailed the hir-

SHADOWS IN THE WIND

ing of extra help, she had found assistance in the form of Arnold Gales, a neighbor, who had served as her hired hand for twenty years. She had then decided to retire and sold the land and cattle some ten years ago, but she did not want to leave the best home she had ever known and had kept a ten-acre plot upon which the house was built. Soon she would have to leave, but not just yet.

The medication had the effect of making Edie drowsy, and she dropped off for a short while. When she opened her eyes she realized that the sun had almost completed its journey to the western horizon. She thought that she should go into the house and make some supper, but the appetite was not there. It was so much more pleasant to sit here and enjoy the evening breeze, inhale the fragrance of spring and watch the purple twilight steal across the landscape, muting the contours of the scene and enveloping her in a sense of well-being. Perhaps it was a false promise, but she knew that she must grasp each moment when so few were left.

After finally forcing herself to eat a small meal, Edie returned to the veranda. Darkness had now descended, and as she settled back into her chair she was struck by the silence that prevailed. Not even the call of the whippoorwill could be heard. In her mind she drifted back to a different time, a time when the farm was a smoothly running entity, with cattle still roaming the meadows. She breathed deeply and could almost smell the smoky fragrance of a smudge fire lit in the early evening of a spring day to ward off the ravenous mosquitoes. She could almost hear the lowing of the cattle as they bedded down for the night or perhaps the voice of a coyote serenading the darkness. The house itself was still, with only the memories lingering there.

A brief moment of sadness touched her thoughts as she recalled that she and Martin had never been able to have children. The meadows had never heard the ringing of childhood laughter, and the galleons of imagination had sailed by on the prairie

YESTERDAY'S SUMMER

breeze with all sails set but no one at the helm. There would be no continuity. Her estate would pass on to a niece who lived in the city some miles distant and was still unaware of the serious nature of Edie's illness. Shortly, perhaps in a couple of weeks, Edie would call her, but not just yet.

Edie had never been overly religious, but now as she looked toward the darkened horizon she could grasp the concept of eternity. It was there in the presence of that pulsating star in the limitless void of space, which seemed to be only inches from a flickering firefly in the back yard, yet was separated by countless light-years and a lifetime of recollection.

The eleventh hour was approaching. Edie knew that she should be seeking her bed, but she was loath to leave this peaceful place as she knew that these times were dwindling. In a few weeks, when she could no longer manage the pain on her own, she would have to enter the nearby hospital for the final battle. In the meantime she would carry on to relive once more a portion of yesterday's summer.

ANDY'S STAR

Charlie felt a small pang of emotion as the car broke over the low ridge and he observed the vista that lay before him. The view from this slight rise in the vast prairie never lost its effect on him. Even after four decades in the mountains of British Columbia, the sight of the old farmhouse set upon the flat tableland a couple of kilometers in the distance to the east awakened in him a feeling of nostalgia. The checkerboard of the fields, broken only by the small bluffs of trees and brush in the wetter areas and the interlacing of the grid roads, stretched toward the horizon in the bright June afternoon. Perhaps the only downer in this scenario was the fact that the house he was looking at was not home. His childhood home had been on the next quarter to the south. No buildings were left there, and the old farmyard had been plowed over. Only a small copse of poplar trees stood near the site of his old home, with a shallow pond nestled within them. No trace remained to show that anyone had ever lived there. The house that was now in his vision, belonged to a childhood friend, Arnold Johnson. Arnold and his wife, Beatrice, made their home here, and Charlie, with his wife, Alice, visited with them at least every couple of years.

Arnold's father, Ben, had built the house almost half a century before. Arnold, as an only child, had inherited it along with four quarters of fairly decent land, including Charlie's old home quarter, which Ben Johnson had bought from Charlie's father, William. Charlie's parents, William and Clara Adams, had retired some three decades earlier to the little town of Williston, which was only a few kilometers away. They had long since passed on and now rested in the small cemetery just outside the town limits. A visit to this peaceful place was always on Charlie's agenda whenever he returned to the area.

Before they made the final leg of the journey to the farmhouse, Charlie and Alice would make a slight detour to the south, to pause for a few moments at the old home site. This was always in Charlie's itinerary, although Alice harbored no great sentiment toward it as she had been born and raised in British Columbia. Charlie would take the time to make his pilgrimage to the old place, to walk a while the pathways of memory to his childhood years. Alice understood his desire to return, if only for a moment, to his roots. The driveway from the access road was still there, and they knew that Arnold and Beatrice would not mind this small trespass, as they too understood his motives.

Parking the car in the driveway Charlie opened the wire gate and they passed through. He was immediately struck by the quietness of the countryside. The perfume of the prairie wildflowers assailed his senses. He remembered the indescribable fragrance of the cowslips, which were the first of the spring flowers to make their appearance. Carpeting the meadows with their orange color, they never failed to dispel those last dregs of a prairie winter. Now, in June, their time had passed and they were gone, replaced by the prairie orchid, the lady's slipper. Later would come the Indian paintbrush and the tiger lily along with a multitude of others he could remember only by their fragrance.

As they entered the home quarter, Charlie allowed his mind to drift again to those long-ago summer days. There was the old thicket, which would later yield the high-bush cranberry, just as he remembered it from times long past. Although he had never been too fond of jam or jelly made from the cranberries, he recalled how much he enjoyed picking them, as well as the wild strawberries, the various mushrooms in season and the gunny sacks full of fat, brown hazelnuts in the fall.

He skirted the copse of poplar trees and approached the now-vacant site of the old house. Only an open field, lying fallow this year, greeted his eyes, but in his mind the house still stood, radiant in a coat of memories, suffused with an aura of remembered warmth and understanding. He closed his eyes for a moment and could almost smell the aroma of homemade bread fresh from the oven that had on many occasions greeted him upon his arrival from school in the afternoon.

Wandering back through the poplars, he spied one old tree, gnarled and twisted, bowing to the years as he would also in the not too distant future. Set within the bark were the initials *C.A. 1949*. Placing his hand upon the inscription, he tried to remember what his thoughts had been when he had carved these initials some five decades before. The veil of the years would not surrender that secret, and he and his wife slowly made their way back toward the car, then drove the short distance to the Johnson farm.

Arnold and Beatrice made their living on this modest farm. It was not large or efficient as modern farms went, but they owed no money on it. Their tractor, as well as most of the other machinery, was many years old, but it did the job of workhorse for the four quarters of land quite well. The house and the other outbuildings were in fairly decent repair. The paved highway passed by a couple of kilometers away, and a gravel road completed the access to the site.

Charlie felt an air of pleasant anticipation as he drove the dusty car into the driveway and leaned on the horn. Today being Sunday, a day of rest, it was only minutes before Arnold and Beatrice emerged from the house. Arnold, in spite of his fifty-nine years, was still looking fit and trim from many seasons of hard work. Charlie, on the other hand, was wearing a slight paunch, no doubt the result of having lived his adult life in the city. Beatrice, looking younger than her fifty-three years of age, always had a smile to welcome them, and Alice, looking slightly wan from a lingering illness, the dark hair showing traces of gray, hurried forward to embrace her. After a round of hugs, handshakes and backslapping, all went inside.

It had been a year and a half since their last visit, and the hours flew by as the old friends recounted the recent happenings in their lives.

"We received your card at the time of Andy's passing," began Beatrice. "We certainly wish that you could have been here. It was a difficult time."

Andy Stewart was Arnold's cousin. Oddly enough, they had only met about four years earlier. Ben Johnson's sister, Mary, had married and moved to the other end of the country long before Arnold had been born. Ben had lost touch with her and her husband over the years, and she had passed on at an early age. Neither Arnold nor his parents had been aware of Andy's existence. Ben and Linda, Arnold's mother, never did find out about it before their deaths some years ago. Arnold and Andy had been reunited through some chance happenings of which Charlie was never fully informed. Over these short years they had become close, and as they were separated by only two hundred kilometers, they spent many pleasant interludes making up for the lost years.

Charlie had met Andy a couple of times, although he never got to know him well. His first impression of Andy was that he did not show a lot of emotion. He had managed a collection agency in the city, and the emotional aspect of that environment was not conducive to acquainting a person with an appreciation of the natural beauty of life. That lifestyle did not instill in him the same country values that were a part of the heritage of the people living off the land. Andy, however, did have a sense of humor. He often liked to tease his wife, Rita, Charlie remembered, while telling her some outrageous tall tale. All the time he would be recounting the story, he would be facing half away from her with only the right side of his face visible to her. Charlie knew that the story was not quite true when he saw Andy's left eye close in a long slow wink.

Sixty-one years of age at the time of his passing, Andy had learned only three months before his death that he had the big C. Ten months ago he had lost his battle. Whatever lay beyond this life was no longer a mystery for Andy. His journey was done.

The conversation flowed easily and the afternoon passed swiftly by. Rising suddenly from her chair, Beatrice exclaimed, "Goodness, it's almost five o'clock. I will start supper. Alice, come and give me a hand. The men can have a drink on the patio while they fire up the barbecue."

Arnold led the way outside with Charlie following. Rolling the charcoal barbecue to an area away from the wall near which it had been stored, Arnold wire-brushed the grill surface and laid the charcoal. Pouring on some fire-starting fluid, he set it alight and stepped back.

"Pour us a short one, Charlie. We can sit and chew the rag while the coals are getting prepared."

Charlie set out the glasses and poured the drinks. Neither he nor Arnold was a big drinker, but a few were always welcome during these visits. They aided relaxation and, at least in Charlie's case, allowed him to remember fondly those days of long ago when the sun seemed to shine ever so much brighter and the clouds of uncertainty and doubt did not even exist. Those golden summers would forever linger in the pictures in his mind.

Sitting back in the well-worn patio chairs was a comfort Charlie never felt in the bustle of the city. The incredible peace of the rural setting never ceased to amaze him. During the occasional pause in the conversation, the only sound to be heard was the chatting of the women in the kitchen. At times Charlie thought that perhaps he was being a rude guest, but he could not help but let his mind wander, to admire the beauty around him, the gaily colored butterflies flitting about, the golden sun lowering in the western sky and the feel of a gentle breeze upon his cheek. All this had been his during the time of his childhood, but somewhere along the journey through the corridors of time it had been lost.

Pushing aside the remains of a delicious steak, Charlie gratefully accepted a steaming cup of coffee from Beatrice. Dessert was a luxury he could ill afford. He took a sip of the steaming brew and leaned back.

"That was a wonderful meal, Beatrice. I can't remember when I've enjoyed better."

"Why, thank you, Charlie. Arnold and I are certainly glad that you and Alice could come this year. We do so look forward to your visits."

"We love coming here," replied Alice. "We regret not being here for Andy's funeral, but with my being in the hospital at the time it was just impossible."

Arnold gazed at the far horizon, for a moment lost in thought. "Andy grew to love this area in the short time that we knew him. He could not bear to be buried in the city. One of his final wishes was that he could rest here in the countryside. He was cremated and his ashes were interred in a plot at the Williston cemetery, not too far from your mom and dad, Charlie."

The conversation shifted to more pleasant topics, and the sun continued its slow descent toward the western horizon. Eventually twilight settled over the landscape, blanketing the land in a purple mantle of shadow. The haunting call of a whippoorwill brought a

ANDY'S STAR

lump to Charlie's throat. The occasional flicker of a firefly could be seen in the velvet dusk.

To the north of the house, a line of evergreen trees was visible in the gathering gloom. Ben Johnson had planted them there even before he had built the present farmhouse. A gap existed between two of the trees, and a single star made its presence known in the night sky, framed by the silhouettes of the two spruce trees. The outside light had been turned out to thwart the mosquitoes, and the moon would not appear on the eastern horizon for another hour. Charlie became aware of the star, shimmering, iridescent, the colors changing in an irregular pattern from turquoise to jade to red or yellow with an occasional burst of white. For a moment its beauty transfixed him and his eyes remained riveted to it.

Beatrice noticed the direction of his gaze. "There's Andy's star."

"Why do you call it Andy's star?" asked Alice.

Arnold took it upon himself to explain. "In the few years I knew Andy, I got to know him quite well. I know that he never seemed to be too emotional, but he did have a soft spot. He went through life looking for the main chance, usually overly concerned with his business. He never stopped to admire the beauty of the natural world, especially that which exists in the night sky. Living in the city, he never saw much of the night sky, what with the lights and all. It was only after he became ill that he began to appreciate the wonder of it all. This star captured his attention on an evening much like this one. The last time he was here, which was about two months before his death, he would spend an hour or two on the patio in the evenings, marveling at the magic of the night. The star was his favorite. Even after everyone went to bed, he would sit here with a pair of binoculars, studying the heavens, trying to make up for lost time I suppose. He was still optimistic when he left that he would beat his cancer. He had hoped to return again, not knowing that on his next visit he would stay forever."

The evening passed quickly, the flow of shared conversation covering all segments of their individual fond memories, mutual dreams, achievements and failures. When 11:30 arrived, Alice was the first to say, "I hate to be a spoilsport, but I'm afraid I'm going to have to turn in. Age is getting the best of me and I can't weather the late nights like I used to."

Beatrice showed her to her room, although this was unnecessary as Charlie and Alice had used the same spare bedroom many times before. Arnold and Charlie continued their conversation for another thirty minutes until Arnold, too, announced that his bedtime had arrived.

Charlie, for some reason he could not fathom, was not tired. Perhaps his six decades of life were beginning to weigh upon his thinking, and, like Andy, he was realizing he too should make up for lost time. He said his goodnights to the others and decided to sit there on the patio for a short while longer. Picking up the bottle from the patio table, he poured himself a drink and settled back in his chair to contemplate the universe and try to solve its secrets.

Charlie sipped his drink. Totally relaxed, he watched the star in the distance. Random thoughts passed through his mind. Andy had found, at the end of his life, that he had missed many of life's pleasures that were free for the taking, available to all. Charlie also realized that perhaps he had missed the many opportunities to savor the simple pleasures, to stop and smell the roses before the coming of winter laid them all to rest. He found himself looking more at the road behind than any road that lay ahead. Sometime it was an illness or the coming of age at last that altered a person's thinking in a way that allowed him, or her, to recognize that life was more than business and the pursuit of the almighty dollar. He wondered if Andy had found the secrets that he had sought in the final weeks of his life.

ANDY'S STAR

The star continued to pulsate, turquoise to jade to red to yellow to white. Suddenly it seemed to pause, the white color engulfing it for an unusually long time, like a long, slow wink. Then it began to pulse again, turquoise to jade to red to yellow to white. Charlie rubbed his eyes. He picked up his glass, now half full. He looked at it then back at the star. Placing his unfinished drink on the table, he rose from his chair and went to seek his bed.

WHEN THE WIND WAS FREE

Wistfully looking out the window at the brilliant blue of the August sky, the five-year-old boy tugged at the collar of his shirt. He was anxious to change from these constricting Sunday dress clothes and run outside into the sunshine, to frolic with his friends, to ride the range with his heroes, those stalwart giants of the silver screen that he had watched only the night before. His mother, however, insisted that he wait until after the noon meal, when the usual weekly family get-together was in progress and all were relaxing after a good meal. Two hours until dinnertime, almost forever. The tantalizing aroma of roasting chicken permeated the house. An errant summer breeze wafted through the room, fluttering the pages of the calendar that showed the year: 1954. From the old Marconi radio came the golden sound of a choir singing "Rock of Ages." His mother was sitting in the big rocking chair, the Bible in her hands.

"Blessed are the meek, for they shall inherit the earth."

"Rubbish," thought Geordie, settling back in the window seat of the airliner as he watched the runway drop away. "Who would want it, this den of iniquity, this cesspool of corruption?" The sudden pang of memory stirred him deeply across the decades of time. He felt the thump of the landing gear settling into the wheel wells, streamlining the aircraft and making it one with the air, soaring on the wind. Hawaii was the destination, a return to paradise after a hiatus of almost ten years.

After a short period of time the hostess walked slowly along the aisle taking drink orders. Geordie ordered a double scotch.

A lifting of the spirits would be most welcome. When the drink arrived he sipped tentatively and felt the warm glow spread throughout his being. Glancing once more out the cabin window, he saw the checkerboard of the flat prairie spreading far below, reaching for a distant horizon that was obscured by the shimmering heat waves of an unusually warm September afternoon. January would probably be a more optimum time to make this journey, but for him the choice was governed by circumstance. Now was the time.

As the sun began its slow journey toward the western horizon, the huge aircraft sped onward. The cabin interior was relatively quiet with the thunder of the engines following far behind, leaving a trail only those still bound to the earth could hear. Geordie, halfway through his second drink, was oblivious to the presence of his fellow passengers, who were almost all excited at the prospect of a long-awaited vacation. He sat immobile, eyes riveted to the small opening of the window, gazing at the unfolding scene so far below. His thoughts were also far away, in another place, in another time.

He lay there on his back in the soft grass, looking at the low ridge of hills in the distance. The heat waves of a July afternoon were dancing in his vision, seemingly the only sign of life on this vast prairie. The shade of the oak tree was certainly welcome in the heat of the day. The flutter of the oak leaves signaled the presence of the eternal prairie breeze, a buffer against the furnace of the sun. The butterflies frolicked in the sunshine, a songbird sang his melody from a nearby tree and an occasional dust devil weaved its way across the meadow before disappearing from view. All was well in his seven-year-old world. Dreamily he watched the passing of a silver airliner far above him. One day, he vowed, he would ride a craft like the one he saw now, traveling to exotic places, experiencing the best of times. He would be the master of his universe. He felt the breeze ruffle his hair even as it did the oak leaves, a soothing balm in the lazy afternoon.

Emerging abruptly from his reverie, Geordie looked around him. Laughter and good times were the order of the day. The flight was not quite full, so he sat alone, an island of solitude in a sea of good cheer. Seated in an aisle seat across from him and slightly ahead was a comely woman of early middle age. She was sipping a drink, and stealing covert glances in his direction, smiling whenever she felt that he had noticed her. Geordie smiled once, raised his glass in salute and sat wearily back. Taking another sip from his drink, he closed his eyes momentarily. The years fell away, taking him down that long trail of the fifty years of his life.

Hawaii, this was the culmination of his dream. After so many years of struggle, Geordie felt that he had finally arrived. His building-supply business had prospered, money was no longer in short supply and only the best of everything would do at this moment in his life. In 1989 he was a long way from the dreams of his seven-year-old self. Single at forty years of age, perhaps now would be the time to seek a lifetime partner, someone to share his plans with, someone who would stand beside him to weather any storms life had to offer, someone who would provide the quiet harbor for his ship of dreams.

He saw her first in the mirror behind the bar as he sat sipping a drink, awaiting the departure time of his flight. She also sat alone and seemed to be studying him in the reflected image. Their eyes locked and she smiled at that moment. Geordie realized that he was looking at a beautiful woman, probably in her mid twenties. She did not turn away and he decided to try to strike up a conversation.

"I'm Geordie Danton. I leave on flight 309 to Hawaii in forty minutes. I'd be pleased to buy you a drink."

For only a moment she gazed pensively. "What a coincidence. I'm taking the same flight. My name is Joan Wethers and I'll take you up on that drink."

The intervening time passed quickly, a pleasant interlude of camaraderie. Their flight was soon announced, and upon boarding they realized that their assigned seats were only three rows apart. After some negotiation with the stewardess and another passenger, they managed to seat themselves side by side. Again the hours flew by on the wings of mutual interests, shared confidences and carefree laughter. Suddenly Honolulu lay below them. Off in the distance stretched the blue Pacific Ocean, the breakers clearly visible as they ended their journey on the beach.

By the time the aircraft touched down on the runway, Geordie was smitten. He knew that he must see this woman again. As they went their separate ways at the airport terminal, Geordie and Joan arranged to meet on the following morning and tour the island together.

Geordie laid his gold card on the counter of the car rental agency. "I'd like a car for seven days. I have some sightseeing to do, and the scenery is much more spectacular than I had thought." Somehow he sensed that palm trees and white sand were not what he had in mind. As he drove to his hotel, the fragrance of exotic flora reminded him of the perfume she had worn, elusive yet refreshing. Tomorrow promised to be wonderful.

It dawned on Geordie that although he had been looking out the window of the airliner, the scene he had been viewing was only in his mind. Visible outside the aircraft was a broad expanse of cloud interspersed with occasional vistas of a gray ocean far below. He returned again to that time ten years before. He saw again the face of the woman of his dreams, the sparkling smile, the flashing eyes, the infectious laughter and the sunshine that seemed to follow in her footsteps. He remembered the fire in the nights, beginning with that night in Honolulu that inflamed his desires and set the course. There would be no turning back. He remembered the woman who, after some months, became his wife.

First the months, then the years, flew by after their marriage. Geordie and Joan lived their life to the fullest. They bought an acreage outside the city limits and built their dream home on this site. Geordie was hardly aware of the fact that his wife was fifteen years his junior. He was a firm believer in daily physical exercise and kept himself fit. He could not be happier. Joan seemed perfectly content as well. The only thing that marred their union was the absence of children on the scene. Both wanted a family, but after several years of trying they reluctantly concluded that they were doomed to failure in this regard. Geordie applied himself to the business. As it grew it reached a point where he felt that he should expand, but he needed a partner, someone who would share the workload and also inject some fresh capital into the venture.

Ron Bennet was about ten years younger than Geordie. Clean-cut and fit, he presented an impressive figure as Geordie eyed him across the desk. After studying his credentials, Geordie found that he was well-suited to the position of junior partner in the firm. He also met the financial requirements necessary for his entry into the company. Forty-nine percent of the business would be his, while Geordie would still have the final say with his slight majority ownership.

"Welcome to the firm, Ron," Geordie said as he rose to shake his hand. "With the increased capital I'm certain that there is a bright future for this company. By the way, Joan and I are having a barbecue this Saturday. Why don't you come out to the home place and meet the wife." They left the office and entered the main store, where Geordie introduced Ron to the rest of the staff.

79

A sense of déjà vu flitted through Geordie's mind as he saw the city of Honolulu below him. The past decade ceased to exist. Perhaps it was all a dream. Taking a cab to the hotel, the same hotel where he had stayed ten years ago, he checked in and went directly to his room, the same room, which he had managed to book on short notice. Although the room had, no doubt, been refurbished several times since his last visit, the view from the window was the same and the memories flooded his consciousness. When he closed his eyes, he could swear that the fragrance of her perfume still lingered in the tropical evening. He threw his suitcase on the bed. He did not bother to unpack.

Geordie poured himself a stiff drink and settled back in the armchair. With unseeing eyes he gazed at the blue Pacific stretching toward the horizon, a distant horizon, as distant as the thoughts within his mind.

"Hello, Ron, welcome to our home." Joan smiled as she shook Ron Bennet's hand.

Ron smiled in return as he held her hand perhaps a bit longer than was necessary. "I am pleased to meet you, and I'm sure that this business venture will benefit us all."

"I'll let Geordie show you around the homestead while I begin the preparations for supper." With a last calculating glance at her guest, Joan turned around and started for the kitchen.

Geordie closed his eyes and rubbed a hand across his forehead. There had been many Saturday afternoon barbecues, some with the entire store staff and others with only the three of them. Joan had enjoyed them as much as he had. The business prospered under the combined management of Geordie and his new partner. He couldn't have imagined life being any more perfect.

"Geordie, buddy," said Ron one Friday afternoon, "I was won-

*dering ... As you seem to prefer to tie things up on Friday after-
noons, I thought that I might hit the old golf course. My game has
been slipping somewhat lately, and this might be an opportunity
to brush up on my technique."*

"Certainly, Ron," replied Geordie. *"I rest easier on the
weekend if I know that all the loose ends have been tied up for
the week."*

Pouring another drink, his fourth since he entered the room,
Geordie remembered again those Friday afternoons when his
partner was on the golf course. Especially he remembered that
Friday afternoon of two days ago. He remembered it vividly.

*Friday afternoon, three thirty to be exact. Geordie realized that
he had left the house that morning without some vital written
information that he would need to finish the day's paperwork.
"Oh well," he thought, "I'll bring it in on Monday. It's nothing
that can't wait."*

*Closing the office door, he passed by the receptionist's desk.
"Judy, I'm leaving early. There is nothing special outstanding on
the agenda, and I'll leave the lockup to you. See you on Monday."
He walked to his vehicle and drove away.*

*Approaching the house, Geordie realized how secluded his
property was from the surrounding homes. Funny, but this was
the first time that had registered. The driveway was shaded by
the linden trees that bordered its length. Suddenly he saw that
a vehicle was parked near the house. On closer inspection he
realized that the vehicle was an suv, much like the one driven by
his partner, Ron, who should be at the golf course miles away. A
chill of apprehension caused Geordie to shiver.*

*Parking his car some distance from the house, he proceeded
up the driveway on foot. Gently trying the front door, he found it
locked. He softly inserted his key, opened the door and stepped*

inside. Nobody was in sight. He paused to listen. Muted sounds descended the staircase from the upstairs bedroom. There was no doubt in Geordie's mind what these sounds were.

A terrible rage gripped his being, enveloping him with a sense of betrayal and pain. Quietly he walked to his den. Again using a key, he unlocked the drawer of the desk and opened it, exposing a .38 revolver, unregistered, that he used for some occasional target practice. This weapon was a legacy from his great-uncle, and Geordie had been unwilling to get rid of it. Lifting it from its resting place, he loaded it carefully and made his way up the stairs.

Stopping for a moment outside the bedroom door, Geordie felt like he was in a trance. This could not be happening to him. His perfect world was in ruins, and it was not he but a stranger who stepped through the bedroom door. For only a few moments he saw the thrusting bodies on the bed, thrusting first in the throes of passion, then in time to the jolting of the .38 slugs slamming into them.

He took one last long look and turned away, gently closing the door behind him. Placing the revolver on a coffee table in the living room, he sat in the armchair for several minutes in total shock. His world had crumbled; all was lost.

Entering the bathroom, he splashed cold water on his face, retched dryly into the sink, and opened the medicine cabinet to see if anything was available to settle his queasy stomach. His gaze fell on a medicine bottle. He picked it up and saw that it was a bottle of sleeping pills, almost full, that had been prescribed for his wife some months back when she had suffered from recurring insomnia. He read the label, "Only one per day, definitely no alcohol." He remembered that the pills had not agreed with her, and she had taken only two.

A knowing look came upon his face, as though a decision

had been made. Pocketing the container, he returned to the living room and dialed a number he had not used in a while, the one for his travel agent. After imparting some explicit instructions, he hung up the telephone and walked to the thermostat. Adjusting the air-conditioning to the maximum setting, he exited the front door, carefully locking it behind him.

Geordie refilled his glass once more. He removed a thin envelope from his suitcase. Opening it, he looked at the pills within. Bringing them to Hawaii had been simple. He had simply taped the envelope to his calf, not really caring if it was found or not. Only a cursory check of his luggage had been made. One by one he swallowed the pills, washing them down with the remainder of his drink. He lay back on the bed and closed his eyes.

Here in paradise it began. Here it would end. For a moment Geordie was aware of the hum of the air conditioner. He felt the small breeze caress his cheek. Funny, he thought, how much that breeze was costing him. Having charged the flight and these accommodations to his platinum credit card, he did not know if the airline or the hotel would ever collect. He did not really care. His mind drifted slowly back through the decades to a place on the prairie, to the innocence of childhood, to a time when the wind was free.

At last! Dinner was over. The five year old changed quickly into his overalls. With no shoes on his feet he ran out the door and across the meadow. He felt the freshening breeze ruffle his hair. He ran with the freedom of the wind. He felt as though he could run forever. As he glanced about he saw no butterflies frolicking in the sunlight. No songbird sang from the trees nearby. Suddenly he was tired, oh so tired! Perhaps he would just lie here on the cool grass for a few moments, close his eyes and let the wind scatter his troubles to the four corners of his limited world. He did not see the dark storm cloud approach; he did not hear the crash of the thunder as the lightning flashed around him. The black funnel descended and carried him away.

A BOX OF MEMORIES

It was a simple little sign. Standing on a concrete base and measuring about a meter high by three meters wide, it was constructed of cedar planks and was almost obscured by the neatly trimmed hedge that surrounded the spacious property. All that appeared on its natural wood surface were the words *SEPTEMBER SONG*. Modest though it was, it said all that needed to be said. Anyone who was at all familiar with this section of the city knew it for what it was, a retirement home, a full-care nursing facility for those who had passed the point where they could do for themselves and now must rely on others to aid them in their journey toward the coming winter.

With spacious grounds and a tidy ornamental garden complete with benches that always seemed to be vacant, it had a quiet air proclaiming the presence of those who had reached the late September of their years, so much like the autumn season, the hush before the advent of the bitter cold. An errant breeze with an icy cutting edge lazily swirled the falling leaves in the last rays of a setting sun, ever so much like a mad custodian who could never quite decide where to put them. The snowcapped mountains in the distance glowed in the fading light. Already the lights inside were visible on the shady side of the rambling structure, glowing with a promise of warmth and security within.

The muted patter of soft-soled shoes could be heard in the brightly lit hallway as the two caregivers made their way along. Sandra, middle-aged and graying at the temples, with the wrinkle lines of her stress-filled occupation etched on her face, was imparting instructions to her younger counterpart as they walked along. Judy, twenty years of age with a glowing look of anticipation imprinted on her features, eager to learn the ins and outs of her chosen profession, was hanging on to every word.

"It's a shame, it really is. Look around at the facilities — comfortable rooms, excellent recreation area with two pool tables that are hardly ever used, a large-screen television that is seldom turned on, a common dining room for those who are capable of leaving their rooms for their meals, even though half of these people will not remember what they ate, and last but not least, a full complement of professional caregivers who must surrender themselves to the fact that they can only make a difference in the short term, with the final result sadly inevitable." Sandra paused here as they met two of the resident seniors taking a last stroll before bedtime.

The two ladies shuffled along slowly. Neither would ever see eighty again. Martha, diminutive, with graying hair and a faraway expression in her eyes, said wistfully, "I can't wait for my holiday. We are going to Italy, you know. George is looking ever so forward to seeing the places where he was stationed during the war. We plan to take a lot of pictures."

Martha's companion looked straight ahead as she pushed her walker forward. Marie's gaze seemed to be focused on a nearer horizon. "I must get home soon. I have so much housework to catch up on. Martin simply can't get along without me there to look after him."

Sandra and Judy smiled and nodded at the elderly women as they met, but the older ladies passed by without appearing to notice the younger pair. Sandra glanced at Judy and said in a wistful tone of voice, "Martha and Marie, just two people of the many you will meet here. Both their husbands have been gone for years, but they continue to live in their own little world, seeing some

A Box of Memories

distant horizon visible only to them. Oh well, I suppose the dream is better than the reality."

Judy smiled sadly as she replied, "It is hard to fathom the meaning of it all, but we must do our best to ease their final days however we can."

They continued along the hallway, glancing into each doorway as they passed. Many of the residents were already in their beds, some voluntarily while others were there on a semi-permanent basis, leaving the bed only with assistance from one of the caregivers. They finally arrived at a small room at the very end of the building. The sign at the side of the door said *Charles Sinclair.*

Sandra paused briefly to peer into the room. A frail elderly gentleman was reclining upon his bed, seemingly asleep. A sickly, yellow hue showed on his face, which at this time was the only part of his body not covered by the sheets. After watching for a short interval, Sandra turned and began to exit the room.

"It looks like Charlie is out for the night. We'll check on him in about four hours. His liver is gone. Too many years of drink. It surely seems like a waste of a human life. He has so little to show for it. His whole existence is summed up in a shoebox. All his personal belongings, except for his few clothes, are kept in a shoebox beneath his bed. He wouldn't hear of our storing them for him, insisted that they stay with him. It's just a collection of junk as far as I can see, but you can understand my point. It is sad to see someone's entire life in a shoebox." Slowly they left the room and continued on their way.

Charlie Sinclair, lying motionless beneath the sheets, was fully aware of their passing. The comment he had overheard did not bother him greatly. He no longer cared. What could they know? His days passed in a rosy feeling brought on by the pain medication he was taking. The meaning of life was now lost to him, but when he had his bad days, which were becoming more frequent, he could retreat into that shoebox, his box of memories. The nurses could not know. They had never lived his life. He did not even have to open the shoebox. He knew every item within by heart. All he had to do when the pain became too great was reach one hand beneath his bed and place it on the shoebox. He could then escape to a place where the pain was not, a place where life was good, a better place in a better time.

Every item in the shoebox was indelibly imprinted on Charlie's mind. To be sure, there were a few items that were only of a passing interest, like the tattered birth certificate needed only to give credibility to his existence, to prove that he was an actual breathing, living person, even if at times he couldn't be absolutely certain of that fact. There was an old car key, a key to the first car that he had owned, a Ford sedan of ancient vintage. The car had long since passed on to that great wrecking yard in the sky, but the key represented the good times the automobile had shared with him, as well as those heady days of youth when the limitless future beckoned. A stained brown envelope lay at the bottom of the shoebox. Within it was a faded old photograph of a man, middle-aged, dressed in a dark suit and sporting a full mustache, and a woman, on the younger side of thirty, smiling for the cameraman. They were Charlie's mother and father, gone now these many years, posed by a substantial house set into a slightly rolling landscape near the edge of a central Saskatchewan town. A towering white cloud was visible in the background of the black-and-white picture. Grainy and soiled as it was, it still could take Charlie back to a time when he could feel the touch of a fragrant prairie breeze ruffling his hair, soothing his yearnings and restoring his youth. Along with these items was a collection of assorted receipts, most of which had long since lost their meaning, an old pawn ticket, a very old pocket watch with a broken face, stopped for all eternity at twenty-nine minutes past four, and a battered gold-plated locket with a broken release mechanism.

Charlie sighed in remembrance. He reached down to rest his hand on the shoebox, and his thoughts commenced their travel, however briefly, into those days of long ago.

Lying back upon the sandy shoreline of that nameless prairie lake, Charlie was in a restless frame of mind. Gazing across the stillness of the mirrored surface, which was only occasionally stirred by a passing August breeze, he weighed his thoughts carefully. At sixteen years of age he felt a yearning to escape this drab existence, to shed the shackles of adolescence, engage that flight of fancy, take the world by storm and make his mark upon it all. When he was done, they would all know that he had passed this way. His father had been urging him to finish his education and join up for a hitch in the military, "to make a man out of him," as he had put it.

Sighing, Charlie arose from his reclining position, picked up a stone and sent it skipping across the water's surface, watching it deflect several times, leaving ever-decreasing ripples before it sank into its watery grave. Exactly the opposite of this would be his life, moving upon the waters of chance with ever-increasing effect until the final moment, when he could settle gracefully into his final rest knowing full well that he had given his all.

That year, 1936, which held only despair and hopelessness for so many, meant little to Charlie. His father was the banker in the nearby town, and the hard times had mostly passed them by. Charlie paused for a moment as he eyed the 1932 Ford car parked on the shoulder of the nearby gravel road. Although used, it had been an exciting gift from his father on the occasion of his sixteenth birthday. His mother had not approved. It had seemed to her too much of an extravagance in this time of want for so many. Charlie was confident that this car would be his key to good times. He was popular among most of his peers, and he already had his eye on Millie, a sixteen-year-old farm girl of exceptional beauty and a ready wit. The future would be his. Nothing could hold him in check.

Darkness had descended outside the window of Charlie's room. Opening his eyes for a few moments, he gazed about at his sterile surroundings, everything so neat and proper, a place for everything and everything in its place. He could feel the return of a dull pain within his being. It would soon be time for his medication. Perhaps it was better to lock out the present and retreat once more into that time of long ago when the fire still flowed within his veins and the horizon was still so far away. For a time he could shut out the cold, that damnable cold.

Standing on the edge of the tarmac in the twilight glow of a sun just now disappearing below the horizon, Charlie Sinclair watched the enormous black aircraft before him. It seemed odd, he thought, that although he had completed twenty-eight operations as pilot of this Lancaster bomber, it was as though he was seeing it for the first time. Dwarfed by the magnificent war machine, he remembered his earlier flight training in the much smaller twin-engine Bolingbroke over the flat prairie of Saskatchewan and the rolling foothills of Alberta. He gazed at the nose art on this great beast. Painted on the nose was a fierce black bird outlined in red. The legend it bore in matching red letters was "The Great Black Bird." It gazed back at him with a malevolent eye on this November evening of 1943. Charlie was certainly grateful that they were on the same side. It would soon be time to depart upon their mission. Ominous black clouds were visible over the English Channel, obscuring the eastern horizon; east where lay the industrial heartland of the enemy.

Straining to lift the thirty-ton weight of aircraft, fuel and

A Box of Memories

armaments from the runway, the Packard Merlin engines filled the sky with their throaty roar alongside thirty-four other aircraft in the tightly grouped bomber unit. Making a wide circle to the west to gain altitude before departing to the coast of France, they made a formidable sight.

Charlie relaxed somewhat as they began their journey. He knew that there was little chance of attack here over the channel. The enemy's air force had been greatly depleted over the previous months, and the real threat would come much nearer the target area. Charlie allowed his thoughts to drift as, subconsciously, he went through all the motions of flying the war machine. He knew he had a competent crew, all prairie boys except for Andre, who hailed from a small town in Quebec. Andre occupied the mid upper gunner's position. He spoke with a decidedly French Canadian accent and was seldom caught unawares. Ray, the rear gunner, with his boyish grin and unruly brown hair, had grown up not two hundred miles from Charlie's home and now occupied the loneliest spot on the aircraft. Arnie the navigator, George the wireless operator, Norman the bomb aimer and front gunner, and Les the flight engineer completed the tightly knit group. Charlie, at twenty-three years of age, was at least three years senior to the next oldest of the group, but the aging of combat experience was evident in the eyes of all.

Charlie gazed out the windscreen of the aircraft. A three-quarter moon occasionally broke free of the darkened banks of cloud cover to reveal a limitless void of black sky pinpointed by a myriad of twinkling stars. It was difficult to absorb the presence of so much beauty on a mission of destruction.

The aircraft entered a thick black cloudbank and Charlie lost sight of the others in the group. Maintaining speed and position meticulously, they flew onward through the darkness. Suddenly a brilliant flash erupted from the gloom ahead of, and slightly above, the Black Bird. Charlie knew immediately what had happened. Two of the bombers had collided, and his main concern now was to avoid the resulting debris.

The bomber shuddered, then faltered as an unseen object struck it somewhere on the starboard wing. The plane lost power and Charlie realized that the outer starboard engine had stalled. Les quickly shut off the fuel supply to the stricken engine. Charlie increased the throttles on the remaining three to compensate. The clouds parted for a few moments and the pilot and flight engineer could see the blackened hulk of the engine, the propeller missing, and a hole in the wing as well. The aircraft responded to the controls although sluggishly. Turning back was out of the question. They would continue on their mission but they would choose the alternate target nearer home. Charlie knew they would be extremely vulnerable to an attack by the JU 88 night fighters that they had been encountering on recent missions.

Still thirty minutes from the alternate target area, the Black Bird flew on alone, laboring on its three remaining engines, far below its usual ceiling, with both the pilot and the flight engineer scanning the gauges constantly, ever on the watch for further malfunctions as they neared the target, a major railway yard. It was time to drop their bomb load and quickly depart.

The aircraft rocked to and fro from bursts of flak as they passed over the drop site. Charlie steadied the crippled aircraft as best he could. The bombs-away signal came from the bomb aimer, and all felt the bomber lift as the load was released. Without pausing to check on the results, Charlie banked the lightened aircraft and began the homeward journey. All eyes on board were scanning the perimeter of whatever piece of the night sky lay within their vision, all anxiously hoping for a miraculous escape from the JU 88s, the werewolves of the night.

Charlie's headset crackled to life as he heard the tail gunner

A Box of Memories

exclaim, "Fighter, five o'clock low, coming in fast." The stuttering rapid fire of the rear-mounted machine gun bracketed the comment. The bomber bucked beneath the onslaught of the 20-millimeter cannon fire coming from the JU 88 night fighter. Charlie's evasive maneuvers were severely limited by the reduced capacity of the airplane's engines. He merely pulled the craft into a shallow dive. At the same moment he felt a blow like a sledgehammer as something struck his shoulder. A shell had hit the only piece of armor plating on the aircraft, just behind the pilot's position, and a piece of shrapnel plowed a deep groove across Charlie's shoulder. With blood streaming profusely from his wound, he braced himself against the shock and attempted to maneuver the craft with the assistance of the flight engineer, who had quickly grasped the gravity of the situation.

The fighter pilot miscalculated their response, and as he passed above the bomber for a quick turnaround to attack what he thought would be a bomber descending rapidly in the classic corkscrew maneuver, he left himself exposed momentarily to the watchful eye of the nose gunner. As the fighter passed, the staccato bark of the machine gun could be heard. A trail of tracer fire arced across the midnight sky toward the black shadow of the JU 88 until they merged and the fighter erupted in a ball of flame. The Great Black Bird roared on into the night.

Tense minutes passed as two pairs of eyes in the cockpit anxiously watched for any more indications of vital damage. Charlie, fighting the pain, attempted to raise the tail gunner on the intercom but could get no answer. Andre advised on the intercom that he would check on Ray's situation. Les, the flight engineer, quickly summoned George, the wireless operator, to administer first aid to Charlie's wounds. After a time they realized that they were losing altitude, albeit slowly. To ditch the aircraft either here, over enemy-held territory, or in the North Sea was not an

SHADOWS IN THE WIND

option. Survival would be highly unlikely. Charlie decided that they would ride it out to the end, either home or eternity.

The hours dragged by with Charlie using every bit of his skill to nurse the wounded bird along. No more fighter aircraft had been sighted, and the mid turret gunner had made his way to the tail end of the plane and reported that the rear gunner, although still alive, had been severely wounded by shrapnel. He would do whatever he could to stabilize the man.

The channel crossing was nearly over and the shadowed coast of England was showing in the moonlight. The clouds had departed and the runway was now in sight. Charlie dropped the landing gear. A red light glowed on the dashboard, indicating a problem with the starboard landing gear. A visual check by the flight engineer confirmed that the wheel assembly had descended, but perhaps it was not locked. By this time the fuel supply was critically low. There was nothing to be done except to make the landing attempt.

The outer port engine sputtered and stalled, followed immediately by the inner starboard one. Just as the wheels touched the tarmac the last engine sputtered and died. The starboard landing gear collapsed, and the aircraft skidded down the runway, making an arc toward the right of the field. The screeching of metal was almost unbearable, and the shower of flame lit up the night. The wounded bomber came to rest in a farmer's field adjacent to the runway. The resulting flames flickered and died. There was no fuel left to burn.

Charlie's mind slipped slowly into oblivion. He did not see the ambulances hurriedly approach the stricken aircraft. The Great Black Bird had come home for the last time.

Charlie's thoughts quickly reverted to the present as he realized that the pain was becoming more intense. He reached over and pulled on the cord intended to summon the night nurse. Briefly

A BOX OF MEMORIES

he remembered the aftermath of that long-ago night. All the crew had survived. Only after the completion of the flight had it become evident that Andre, too, had been grievously wounded in the attack. Charlie had been rotated home to finish the war as a flying instructor. He had also been awarded the Distinguished Flying Cross. For many years it had sat upon his mantelpiece with several other associated service medals, polished till they shone, only to eventually fade like all dreams do.

Charlie closed his eyes momentarily as Sandra entered the room pushing the small trolley ahead of her, pausing only to switch on the overhead lights.

"Feeling uncomfortable, Mr. Sinclair?" Sandra began as she hastened to the bedside. "We'll have you right as rain in a jiffy." She began to prepare the hypodermic to administer the painkiller.

Charlie attempted to smile but only managed a grimace as the needle penetrated his skin.

"In a few minutes things will look a whole lot better," continued Sandra as she held Charlie's hand while she checked his pulse. "I will be going home now, but Lois will be taking over the next shift. Don't hesitate to call if you need assistance." Just before she left the room she refilled his water pitcher on the bedside table.

The minutes passed and Charlie could feel the effect of the medication kick in. A feeling of well-being enveloped him, distancing him from this person in the bed. Charlie knew full well that the effects would last for only a few hours, but he would take every moment he could. He knew that sleep would be a long time coming to the weary body, and the mind could still travel where it may. He lay with his eyes closed and tried to will away the present. The past was ever so much more acceptable.

The years rapidly slid away. Charlie vividly remembered

95

those post-war times. Euphoria was perhaps the only word to describe the aftermath of the terrible war. He was able to rise each morning free of the fear of what the day would bring, to revel in a prosperity undreamed of just scant weeks before, and to plan for a future that looked so bright with promise. Surely, he had thought then, there would only be the best of times.

It was great to be home again, to awaken each day knowing that death and destruction did not lurk around every corner. Charlie knew that he should be formulating some concrete plans for his future, but it was so pleasant just to relax for a short while, perhaps to bask a bit in his new found standing in the community since the end of the war. Millie had waited for him, and he knew for certain that she would be a large part of his life.

"Charlie, we need to talk," Wilbur Sinclair, Charlie's father, began as they pondered the coming day over a morning cup of coffee. "I don't know if you've given much thought to what you will be doing now that you're out of the air force, and I don't believe that you will be satisfied with just a regular job. Getting a business of your own is probably the way to go. I know that Stanley Morton is considering selling his general store. It may not be too prosperous yet, but times are quickly improving and you might do well in that line. I can help you with all the financial arrangements if you'd like."

Charlie sipped his coffee in silence, deep in thought for a few moments. "You may be right," he replied. "I have been thinking along those same lines myself. It certainly would not hurt to approach the man to see what we can work out."

Charlie coughed weakly. Clearing his throat, he reached over to the pitcher and poured some water into the glass on the table beside him. Slowly drinking it down, he thought again about that long-ago time that seemed like only yesterday. In a matter of weeks, as he now remembered, the deal had been made and Charlie had become the proprietor of the general store. Over the next year he brought many improvements to the business, not only expanding his clientele and, consequently, his volume, but also renovating a part of the large building and renting space to both an insurance agent and a barber. The result was that 1946 had been a year of rapidly changing horizons, each more distant yet more easily reached than the preceding. One more event would make his life complete.

July 20, 1947, a day that he would never forget, with a gentle summer breeze blowing from the southwest and only a few white popcorn clouds sailing across a sunlit sky of endless blue. Charlie watched his bride, Millie, as he held the door of the car open for her to enter. Radiant beyond description in her gown of white, wearing a smile to rival the sun itself, she took her seat and turned to wave at the crowd gathered in the yard of the small white church. Charlie could not remember ever being so content. All his hopes and dreams were being realized. The future was theirs and theirs alone.

Charlie glanced at the illuminated face of the clock hung on one wall of his room. Only half an hour past one o'clock, even though it seemed forever since Lois, his caregiver, had checked in on his condition at the start of her shift. The long night still lay ahead and he wished that he could find the oblivion of sleep, yet he knew that time was running out and he should pursue every waking moment left to him. It was funny how the life of promise that he had expected to have had altered so dramatically those many years ago. Destiny, it seemed, played no favorites.

"Millie Karns" was a name he did not think of very often, but that had been his wife's maiden name until he changed it to "Millie Sinclair." After a honeymoon, by train, to the west coast,

Vancouver in particular, Charlie and his new bride had settled into their life together with high hopes and a certainty of success. They had rented a small house near the store, although they knew that this was only a temporary step. The first Christmas had been memorable, with Charlie's parents and Millie's parents receiving the news that they would become grandparents sometime the following July. It was certainly a festive season, a time of great rejoicing.

On this occasion, Charlie and Millie had exchanged gifts. He presented her with a gold-plated locket with a golden chain. Within the locket were pictures of him and her, facing each other from the opposing sides. A spring-activated release mechanism set into one side of the locket allowed access to the pictures inside. She, in turn, presented him with a magnificent old pocket watch. Her maternal grandfather had used this watch for many years when he had worked for the railroad shortly after the turn of the century. Charlie was deeply moved. Usually an heirloom of this sort would be passed on to the eldest male heir, but Millie was an only child so she had received it from her mother on her twenty-first birthday. Charlie knew that he would wear it rarely, only for special occasions, but he would keep it cleaned and serviced yearly, and he was certain, deep within himself, that he would one day pass it on to his son.

The spring of 1948 had come and gone. The hardware business at that time was running exceptionally well. Charlie had put every effort into expanding the store and now was beginning to think that he should break away to spend more time with his wife, making plans for their coming child who, Charlie was sure, would be a son.

The summer had been extremely hot and dry. The date was July 15 and Millie was due to deliver any day now. The heat was not helping any, and her mood had been irritable. Wearily she wiped

A BOX OF MEMORIES

her brow with a handkerchief as she glanced out the window. She could see a thunderhead in the southwestern sky. She was certain that there would be a storm that night.

At 2:00 am, July 16, 1948, Charlie watched anxiously as the doctor stooped over the form of the woman on the bed. Millie had gone into labor at 11 the evening before and Charlie had quickly summoned the doctor to the house. They were now preparing for a difficult birth. Millie's mother, Emily Karns, had arrived the previous evening to help in any way she could, and she now stood by, ready to assist the doctor. Millie's father, Leonard Karns, was not able to be there due to work-related duties at the farm. He would arrive tomorrow. Charlie's mother and father, by some miscalculation of timing, were out of town and would also arrive on the morrow.

Outside the house the storm was unleashing a barrage of light and sound in its fury. The house reverberated with each thunderclap. The shriek of a violent prairie wind echoed through the room. The sky visible through the windows alternated from brilliant daylight to impenetrable darkness with each flash. Morning could not come soon enough to bring relief both to the land and to the suffering woman on the bed.

At 5:30 am the sun was shining through the bedroom window when the urgent cry of a child sounded through the house. The storm had broken an hour earlier and all the land lay fresh and clean with a fragrance that only a summer's morning on the prairie can bring. The sound of an early songbird proclaiming the coming glorious day carried across the stillness. Charlie stood by, looking drained, as the doctor placed the child, a baby girl, into her mother's arms. Charlie was somewhat disappointed that a son had not been born, but he was careful not to let it show. He knew that it was of small consequence. There would be another time. Emily Karns also looked exhausted but wore a glowing smile upon her face.

The next two years passed quickly. Charlie's earlier disappointment turned to joy as he watched his daughter quickly pass through the crawling phase and begin to walk and run, as well as develop the rudiments of conversation. "Summer Dawn Sinclair" was the name they had given her, but for her short years she would carry the name of "Stormy." Tempestuous was perhaps the best way to describe her, passionate about all living things, mercurial, laughing one instant at a brightly colored butterfly, yet crying the next moment at the sight of a dead bird lying by the roadway. The sight of his daughter running through a meadow filled with wildflowers, her golden tresses sailing on a warm spring breeze, the musical lilt of her laughter carrying through the golden morning air, with her dog, Buffy, keeping pace, was to Charlie a joy beyond description.

August 16, 1951, Millie and Stormy were walking by the blacksmith's shop when the sound of thunder echoed in the distance. "What is that, Mommy?" asked the little girl.

"Why that is God in his blacksmith shop," answered her mother. "That is the sound of his hammer on the anvil."

The little girl gazed at the distant storm clouds. "You can even see the sparks when the hammer hits the anvil," she replied.

Charlie shifted his position in the bed, trying to ease the cramps developing in his legs. Feeling slightly better, he allowed his mind to drift once more. He remembered that Stormy had never shown the fear of storms that most children do. Her single greatest joy was to run barefoot through the puddles left behind by a passing summer rain, and she usually had to be restrained from charging out into the downpour. On one occasion, when the lightning was dancing toward the distant horizon, he recalled that she had approached him, eagerly stating, "Daddy, I can hear God's ham-

A Box of Memories

mer. Can we go outside and watch the light?" She had loved the ever-changing, living sky of the prairie.

Another time, about 1952 if memory served correctly, a friend of Stormy's who was a couple of years older than his daughter had asked Charlie, "Mr. Sinclair, what did you do in the war?"

Charlie, not wanting to dramatize the horror of the war years for these children, merely glanced toward the heavens. Seeing a single cloud sailing along on a brisk westerly breeze, he replied, "Why, I rode the wind."

Charlie remembered that the spring of 1952 was when his mother and father, Wilbur and Molly Sinclair, had decided to retire. This was also the year that Charlie and Millie had built their home. Millie, having been raised in the country, was loath to live the rest of her life within the restricting confines of the town. She had convinced Charlie, without a great deal of effort, that they should build their home in the country. They had purchased a quarter section of land just two miles west of the town, and it was here they built their house. Millie's parents were not too keen on this idea and felt that their daughter would benefit from the amenities available in town after a lifetime of struggle on the farm. Millie was adamant, however, and her decision, much to Charlie's delight, had prevailed.

After viewing the now-completed house, Wilbur Sinclair had mentioned that he would not mind spending the next few years in the country himself. After some consultation with his wife and also with Charlie and Millie, it was mutually agreed that Wilbur and Molly Sinclair would also build a house, their retirement home, on this same parcel of land. By year's end the house was built and all settled down to enjoy their rural lifestyle.

May 25, 1953, Charlie and Millie, as well as Wilbur and Molly Sinclair, were seated around the picnic table in the back yard. Conversing in a low tone, they all took a great deal of pleasure in the sight of Stormy frolicking in the yard with her dog. A warm, fragrant breeze carried the promise of good weather for the foreseeable future. All was well in their world.

Stormy, finally tiring a bit, slowed her steps to a walk and wandered over to where they were seated. Buffy lay down at her feet, also happy to rest a little. Stormy looked up at Charlie with a faraway look in her eyes and a deadpan expression upon her face. She said in a quiet voice, "Daddy, when I grow up I will ride the wind, just like you did in the war."

The distant sound of a train whistle intruded on Charlie's thoughts as he lay there, wrenching him abruptly from his reminiscing as the great iron beast made its way purposefully toward some unknown destination along that unseen but not too distant railroad. How harsh was the whistle of the modern diesel locomotive, so different from the whistle of the steam locomotive of his memory. How stirring it had been to sit in the back yard of his prairie home in the twilight of a summer's day and sometimes hear that faraway call echoing plaintively across the endless expanse of shadowed flat land, seeming to voice a call to reach some distant horizon shrouded in the mists of time and distance. He now knew that the call could come no more. The horizon had been reached and surpassed so many years ago.

June 3, 1953, Charlie and Millie took their ease on the back porch as the evening shadows slowly began to settle over the landscape. Stormy played with her dog in the back yard. The sun had just set in a purple blaze of glory, and the haunting call of a whippoorwill could be heard occasionally from nearby. The sound of the steam train's whistle called through the deepening gloom. Charlie looked toward the railroad track a quarter-mile distant. The railroad track actually cut through their property, and they could see the passage of the train from where they sat. Before

A Box of Memories

long he could make out the shadowy form of the train approaching, the headlight growing with each passing moment, the plume of smoke from the stack inky black against the evening sky.

Stormy loved to watch the train whenever there was the opportunity. She left her dog's side for a few moments and bounded up the porch steps.

"Daddy, when can I ride the train? I want to see where it goes down those tracks. It must be a wonderful place."

Charlie looked fondly upon his daughter's eager face as he replied. "One day you will, darling. Soon I will have to go to Edmonton on business. When I come back we will all go for a train ride. I promise."

A flood of anguish swirled into Charlie's mind as he remembered that long-ago day. He had not kept his promise. He had not even been there to protect his little girl when she needed him. He had been absent on that day, that dreadful August day so many years ago, when time stood still.

Charlie waved as he watched Millie drive away. Stormy, her face pressed against the passenger window of the car, waved back. He looked at the sky, cloudless, a brilliant blue with the rising sun only now making its appearance. He knew it would be another scorcher, this August day of 1953. Millie had driven him into town to catch the early-morning westbound train. He would arrive in Edmonton later that afternoon, complete his business with his suppliers the next day and return home on the third day. He hadn't even left yet, but already he missed his family. Sighing he turned and walked toward the waiting passenger car.

With a bit of a lurch the steam engine took up the slack and the train began to move, the rhythm of the wheels quickly picking up speed, with the hypnotic clickety-clack, clickety-clack *sounding in Charlie's ears. Soon they would be passing by his*

103

home, and Stormy had promised to be watching for him. Sure enough, his house was now in sight and there they were, Millie and Stormy, standing in the sun-burned meadow, waving as he passed. Beyond them lay the never-ending fields of ripening grain reaching toward the far horizon. No cloud was visible in the sky and all was still, with no evidence of a single breath of wind. When they were no longer in sight he turned his gaze forward again, reached for his briefcase on the Pullman seat beside him and, after removing the documents within, began to pore over the business at hand. The sun, now well above the horizon and showing a burnished, coppery hue, gazed over Charlie's shoulder as the train fled toward the west.

Charlie shifted his position on the bed. The night was passing by, yet sleep eluded him. What would he do without his box of memories to comfort him in these times of crisis? Reaching one arm beneath the edge of the bed, he placed his hand upon the box. A strange energy flowed through his being. For these few moments the stiffness and the dull pain eased and his thoughts took wing again.

The noon hour had come and gone. Charlie had eaten the box lunch that his wife had packed for the journey. Having returned to his paperwork after lunch, he now raised his eyes momentarily and glanced toward the southern horizon. Surprise showed on his features as he realized how the weather had changed. Gone was the brilliant blue sky, replaced by massive thunderheads, towering ominously with gray curtains of rain hanging from their swollen underbellies. Looking back in the direction from which he had come, he saw that the eastern sky was particularly sullen looking, with cloud masses swirling, rolling and twisting, as if in a torment of agony. Over the chuffing of the steam engine some distance ahead of him, he could detect the occasional roll

A Box of Memories

of thunder. A chill passed through him as he thought of his family left behind. Hopefully the storm would not be too bad. He knew that his mother and father were home. As long as they were under shelter, all would be well. His thoughts turned back to his plans for the coming day.

The hailstones rebounded from the windowpanes of the Pullman car as Charlie's fellow passengers anxiously discussed the present weather conditions. All agreed that this was a storm out of the ordinary. As the afternoon wore on, the weather eased, and as the train pulled into the city of Edmonton, the sun began to shine from its perch in the western sky. To the east, however, the sky was black.

Disembarking from the train with his small suitcase and briefcase in hand, Charlie walked the short distance to the hotel where he usually stayed when he was in the city. He took a room for the night. He knew that he had left instructions with Millie and also his staff at the general store as to where he could be reached. He would have a quick supper and turn in early. He planned to hurry his business as much as possible and return home as soon as he could. He had been giving some thought lately to taking a vacation, although he had not yet told his wife of these plans. It was to be a surprise, a holiday by train to Nova Scotia. He knew that Stormy would be especially excited at this news. She would get her train ride at last.

Waking with a start, Charlie gazed about him in bewilderment before he remembered where he was and realized that someone was rapping firmly on the door of his hotel room. The room was still pitch-dark, and he reached over to turn on the bedside lamp. Glancing at the pocket watch on the table, he saw that the hour was seven minutes before four in the morning. Quickly donning his trousers, he strode to the door and opened it. A stab of appre-hension pierced his being as he saw the uniformed police officer standing at the threshold with his hat in his hand.

"Mr. Sinclair? I am sorry to wake you at this time but I'm afraid I have some very bad news," began the policeman.

Charlie's world quickly crumbled into ruins.

Thursday, August 16, 1953, would always be imprinted in Charlie's memory. A week later he could scarcely recall the fleeting passage of the days. Even now, as he stood gazing at the devastation before him, he could not absorb the reality of the circumstance. Dimly he remembered the policeman at the hotel giving him the news that his family was gone. His mother, his father, his wife and beloved daughter, all gone, victims of a savage beast of nature, a tornado. This was the first time he had laid eyes upon the scene since his return, except for a brief glimpse from the window of the moving train. A sense of unreality had filled him then when he realized that not a building was standing in this place that had so recently been home.

He had laid his life to rest only that morning in that quiet place just on the outskirts of the town. Many of his neighbors and friends had attended, all offering their sympathy and support, but in the quiet hour of a sunlit afternoon he had felt the need to be alone, to touch base with his emotions and attempt to see a purpose to this madness.

Charlie Sinclair reminisced as he slowly wandered about the area that used to be his back yard. It was littered with debris from the devil wind that had claimed all within the confines of the property. If it were not for the foundations that remained, it would be difficult to see just where the two houses had stood. Lumber, roofing and bits of glass were everywhere. Two battered

A Box of Memories

and twisted automobiles reposed in differing positions about a hundred feet apart.

A shiny object illuminated in a flash of light from the bright, lowering sun caught Charlie's attention. It had been partly concealed by a piece of wood and he would not have noticed it except for that brief flash. He stooped and picked it up. Suddenly he realized that he held in his hand the pocket watch that Millie had presented to him in what now seemed another life. Turning it over, he saw that the glass face of the watch had been broken and the hands were stopped at twenty-nine minutes past four. Ironically, this timepiece marked the exact time that life, as he once knew it, had ended. Meaning for him had ceased to exist. Pocketing the watch, he continued with his aimless rambling.

Over the next hour and a half he accumulated several items: a grainy black-and-white photograph of his parents in their younger years, a car key from an old car he had owned, and his case of service medals, still somehow intact. There was little else of interest to him. Slowly he turned and began to walk back toward the borrowed automobile in which he had arrived.

Near the edge of the back yard, Charlie's attention was drawn to a piece of wood comprised of two short pieces of board still nailed together, forming something resembling a cross. One end of one piece had been driven into the ground and it stood there like a miniature monument. At its base lay something shadowed by the wood itself. Reaching down to pick up the object, Charlie realized that it was the locket he had given his wife in happier times. Examining the piece, he saw that it was open. The spring-release mechanism had broken off, and he realized that if he closed the locket, he would never be able to open it again without forcing it. The pictures inside, of Charlie and Millie, were undamaged.

Deep in thought for several moments, Charlie suddenly

straightened, reached into his back pocket and extracted his wallet. Removing a photograph from his wallet, he held it in front of his eyes. For a minute he gazed at the likeness of his daughter, Stormy. Taking a small knife from his pocket, he opened the blade and began to trim the edges of the picture to leave only the head. This was now small enough to fit into the locket. Placing the smiling picture of Stormy into the locket, he snapped it shut. She could rest for eternity cradled in the arms of her mother and father.

Charlie cast a last longing glance at the place that had been home. Buried were the dreams, buried with the rest of his family. He would never return here again. What he would do with the store he did not know. Even Leonard and Emily Karns, his mother- and father-in-law, had been somewhat distant toward him. Although they had not said so in so many words, he was under the impression that they laid the blame for the tragedy at his feet, as they had never been in favor of their daughter making her home here in the country. How could he have known? How could anything have been different? A fleeting image of Stormy danced across his vision, a child with hair of gold playing in the back yard with her dog. How ironic that she had not even ended her days here at her home. He had been told that the search party had found her body half a mile away. There was hardly a bruise upon her. She had been curled up on the earth as though she was asleep.

"Daddy, when I grow up I will ride the wind, just like you did in the war." These words echoed through Charlie's mind. She had ridden the wind, just as she had prophesied, to a faraway place somewhere beyond the horizon. She would never return.

Wrenching his consciousness back to the present by force of will, Charlie glanced wearily at the clock on the wall. Almost 6:30 am, yet he still could not sleep. Through the small window in his room

A Box of Memories

he could see that the shadows outside had begun to pale. In a short time the sun would be making its appearance. Oddly enough, he felt no pain. A dull numbness filled his being. It had been many hours since he had taken his pain medication, yet he did not feel the need of any more. Lois, his caregiver, had checked on him earlier, but he had waved her away, insisting that all was well.

As he lay quietly, he thought of those last years, the years that had passed in a fog of loneliness, denial and despair. After the storm he had endured in a vacuum, doing all tasks like an automaton. The store ceased to hold any meaning in his life, and in a matter of a few months he had put it up for sale. He accepted the first half-reasonable offer that came by. Packing his few remaining possessions, he had moved to the west coast.

Charlie wearily reached over to the bedside table and poured a glass of water, spilling only a little of it in the process. Drinking it down, he closed his eyes for a few moments. The numbness was spreading throughout his body. The pain, strangely, was all gone. Outside the window the shadows would soon be dispelled and the brightness of the morning sun would quickly become more evident. With a touch of sadness he recalled those years at the west coast, the two business attempts that failed largely due to a lack of interest on his part and an acquired dependence on the bottle, the only thing that would ease the pain of his loss. Then came the slow slide down that slippery slope of self-pity that ended only when he had been hauled off to the drunk tank on more than one occasion and was eventually confined to this care home by some forgotten social worker. Perhaps the lowest point of that slide was when he had pawned his case of medals for the price of a bottle of cheap whiskey. He had never thought of redeeming them. He no longer felt worthy of them.

Charlie knew that the door of his room was not barred, yet the door of his life had been barred for some years. Soon, he was certain, he would walk out into that morning sunshine, into a meadow filled with the fragrance of wildflowers, into the sun-drenched air of a prairie summer filled with the trilling sound of songbirds, where a golden-haired child and a dog raced across the great, flat expanse and a young woman waited quietly nearby. They would all be there waiting for him. The bars on the door would open and at last he would be free. Once more he reached down, placed his hand on his box of memories and closed his eyes.

The time was 7:45 am. Lois entered the room for one final check on Charlie's condition before she ended her shift.

"Oh good," she thought. "Charlie has finally dropped off to sleep. How content he looks. This is the first time I've seen him smile in some time."

She looked down and realized with a start that Charlie Sinclair's box of memories had spilled across the floor.

A TOUCH OF RHUBARB

They were an unlikely looking trio, seated around the kitchen table, a shot glass, half full, before each one and a bottle, with a very expensive brand of rye whiskey listed on the label, resting on the wood surface of the table. A closer inspection of the bottle would lead one to wonder why the liquid in the bottle appeared clear, like water, instead of the rich amber color of rye, but certainly this thought did not enter the minds of those present.

A soft evening breeze drifted through the small house; both the east-facing kitchen window and the west-facing window in the living room were open to allow its unobstructed passage through the house to help cool the interior on this unseasonably hot July day on the Sunshine Coast. The house was situated in a secluded area, half surrounded by trees yet with a view west toward the inlet some two hundred yards away. A single arbutus tree, flanked by a number of large spruce trees, was visible through the kitchen window as it swayed slightly in the warm wind. A sense of quiet pervaded the scene.

Murdoch Mcveigh, with a full head of steel gray hair, and still a big man although he would never see eighty-five again, raised his glass to his lips and took a small sip as he looked out at the arbutus tree. Funny, he thought at that instant, how that broad-leaved evergreen triggered a memory of the lowly poplar tree that was more than a thousand miles and a lifetime away.

"Good stuff," he ventured, with no hint of a Scottish accent. The other two people seated at the table did not find this surprising, as they knew that he had been born of Scottish parents in

Manitoba. "This is certainly the elixir of memory."

Mike Mathusek, seated to Murdoch's left, took a sip of his own drink. It tasted almost like good Scotch, not too harsh but with a kick like a Manitoba mule. He was a smaller man, standing perhaps five foot eight. Although he was largely bald, with only a fringe around the back and sides of his head, he still looked trim at sixty-eight years of age with none of the paunch that usually came with the passage of the years. He held his glass in his right hand. His left arm was missing below the elbow, the result of a farm accident on the prairie some forty years earlier — an encounter with a hay baler to be precise. He gave up on farming about two years after that episode and moved to Vancouver, where he found employment with a prominent building company. He had retired from that career just five years ago. As the company did extensive building renovations as well as new construction, he had endured the typical one-armed paperhanger jokes through the years, but he had worked on the administrative side, where the handicap of the missing arm was minimal, and had taken it all with a large grain of salt. He looked first at Murdoch, to his right, and then to Lionel Everret, seated across from him. Raising his glass in a toast he said, "Here's to the old prairie homestead, so long ago and so far away."

Lionel Everret clicked his glass, first with Mike and then with Murdoch. Saying not a word he downed his drink. He felt first the fire of it going down and then the warmth spreading throughout his being. For a few moments his thoughts turned inwards and his mind wandered through the corridors of time to those long-ago days. When he had shaved only this morning he had taken note of the face that looked back at him. At sixty-nine years he suddenly realized that he resembled his grandfather from decades before. He too had been raised on a prairie farm, very near the Mathusek farm. He and Mike had been childhood friends. Lionel had moved

A Touch of Rhubarb

to the west coast a couple of years before Mike, just before Mike lost his arm, and it was, in fact, he who had convinced Mike to make the move as well. He had been employed in the construction industry and had helped Mike get settled in his new career. Over the years they remained close friends, retiring as neighbors less than a hundred yards apart. Both were widowers. Mike had lost his wife, Beth, in a car accident twelve years earlier, while Mildred, Lionel's wife, had passed on from a lingering heart ailment just three years past.

Murdoch Mcveigh, although the eldest of the trio, was a relative newcomer to the group. He had bought a property nearby only three years before. He had been divorced from his wife for twenty years or so. He had grown children, as did Mike and Lionel, but in all cases they lived some distance away and contact was sporadic. The three had been drawn together in a kind of loose camaraderie and spent many an evening sipping glasses of homemade wine and spinning yarns about bygone days. They shared a common heritage, having all been born on the prairie — Murdoch in Manitoba, Mike and Lionel in central Saskatchewan.

Murdoch had been a traveling salesman in his younger years, working for a grocery wholesaler and filling orders for the many stores in the little towns scattered throughout the prairie. He had come west a half century before, but he could still spin tales about his travels, being well-acquainted even with the area where Mike and Lionel had been raised. The names of the prairie towns would roll off his tongue — Hudson Bay Junction, Prairie River, Mistatim, Tisdale, Star City, Pathlow, Crystal Springs, Tway, Bruno, Fulda and myriad others, some still struggling to survive while others were only a distant memory marked by a few foundations and an unkempt cemetery that testified to the fact that people once lived there. Even those prairie skyscrapers, the grain elevators, were mostly gone. Murdoch had followed various paths of enterprise in his later years, but his success was largely due to a shrewd purchase of acreage on the outskirts of Vancouver many years before. When the city had expanded, he was able to sell the property for a tidy sum.

The years were beginning to catch up to him now, and he found that he did not have the enthusiasm for his yard and garden that he once had. He knew that the sands of time were running low in the hourglass of life, but he still enjoyed an occasional drink with his friends and a chance to relive his youthful memories through these sessions. Usually it would only be a glass or two of wine, but this was a special occasion.

Lionel Everret picked up the bottle and replenished the glasses for his two friends and himself. "I'm glad I went that extra mile," he offered. "This surely beats the wine."

"It does for sure," returned Mike.

Murdoch merely sipped and nodded his head. Although this "special blend" certainly meant more to his two friends, especially Lionel, it did, in fact, trigger memories of his younger days, when a liquor store was a rare commodity on the prairie and many people made their own with a little sugar and some fruit.

Lionel rose and opened the door to the refrigerator, taking out a plate of snacks that he had earlier put together, some sliced kielbasa, a few cubes of cheese and some sliced pickles. He remembered the old days when snacks were a must while partaking of "the old moon." It would be taken pure, no mix. Funny, he thought, that in this day and age he would be drinking home-brewed whiskey when the store-bought version was so readily available in the nearby city. This batch was indeed a "special blend."

Mike poured another round. "I haven't tasted moonshine in forty years. Whatever possessed you to make this batch?"

Lionel placed the plate on the tabletop, straightening his

A Touch of Rhubarb

back rather stiffly as a result of advancing arthritis before replying, "Well, you know that I made that trip back home about two years ago. I hadn't been back for about fifteen years. Things sure have changed, let me tell you. Most of the people have gone from the area. The younger ones have pulled up stakes, gone in search of greener pastures, and the old folks are mostly passed on. You have to count the tombstones in the cemeteries to see where they are at now, and it's a long way between neighbors. Seems mighty lonesome by my way of thinking. Used to be a large family on almost every quarter of land, but now you can go for miles before you see chimney smoke.

"I made the effort to visit the old farm while I was down there. Seen your place too, Mike. Not much left. The buildings that are still standing have all silvered with age and have developed a distinct lean in the direction of the prevailing wind. A few more years and they will also be history."

The trio paused their conversation momentarily and sipped on their drinks. They had all heard the prairie wind in their time and they all knew the meaning of forever.

Lionel continued, "The one thing that stood out the most when I looked at the old home site was the rhubarb patch. It and the lilac bushes were the only things that never seemed to change. I still remember the rhubarb from way back when I was a kid. As I looked at it this last time, I realized that it was every bit as robust as ever. I got an urge to pick some. As I was heading back west that day, I picked a garbage bag full of the stuff and put it in the trunk of the car. When I got home I couldn't decide what to do with it. If I froze it I would be eating rhubarb pies for ten years. I got this brilliant idea and put on a batch of rhubarb wine. I didn't really know how it would taste, but as I had been making wine for a few years I thought I would make the attempt. It would be a special wine, a wine with a bouquet of memories.

115

SHADOWS IN THE WIND

"Well, you know, I made the wine. You both tried some last year. It was not a bad wine, but it could not compete with the peach and the grape varieties that are more prevalent in these parts. One day I was visiting George Baxter. He's got a small acreage about ten miles from here. He goes to all the yard sales and auction sales. Has more junk around than I've ever seen. Showed me all the stuff he had out in his garage. I noticed this old copper coil from a still. He couldn't remember where he got it. Didn't even know what it was until I told him. That was where I got the idea. I borrowed the still, cleaned it up, distilled the rhubarb wine and, voilà, we have the elixir of memories, just like Dad used to make."

Mike lifted his glass once again in a toast. "Here's to your dad."

A moment of silence ensued as the three men reminisced a bit. Their fathers had all, at one time, concocted that prairie moonshine, a little bit of warmth in a sometimes unforgiving land.

Murdoch swirled the liquid in his glass, mesmerized by the changing color as the whiskey was illuminated by a ray of sunshine that shot through the west-facing window from a lowering sun sinking towards the waters of the inlet. He recalled that his father, Angus Mcveigh, had liked a social drink too, but he certainly did not let it get in the way of his work. Angus had been a small dour man, fair and courteous with his friends and neighbors but hard as nails when the occasion demanded. Murdoch's mother, on the other hand, was a big woman, big in body and big in spirit, and she toiled tirelessly beside her man to wrest a living from that great, flat land.

Mike grimaced slightly as he felt a twinge of pain in the arm that was no longer there. This happened sometimes, even after all these years. A memory of his own father flashed through his thoughts. William Mathusek, or big Bill as he was more com-

116

monly known, had been a skilful violin player and had liked nothing better than to play at the country dances which were a large part of the social fabric of the prairies some fifty years earlier. Mike had also showed talent for the violin, but the accident had ended that, and it was the loss of his music that he considered the most grievous injury inflicted by the baler. With his right arm he raised his glass to his lips. His father's features were indistinct in his memory, but the sound of the violin was as clear as it ever was.

Lionel Everret thought for a moment, then chuckled. "You know, Dad used to make the moonshine back in the thirties and forties, but did I ever tell you about the time my older sister Lynn was put in charge of the project. As you both well know, the process was usually conducted in a hidden place in the woods. The authorities were pretty tough on anyone they found making shine, but most people viewed it as only a social exercise, although they took great pains not to get caught. You remember that Lynn was sixteen years older than me. This episode took place when she was fourteen, so I wasn't even here yet.

"Apparently Dad had a batch on the fire. The fire was small and carefully tended. The cooker was on a metal stand above the flames. I guess it needed careful attention to keep the flames just at the right temperature to keep the process going without blowing the lid off. Mother brought him word that he needed to attend to some chore in the nearby town. I can't exactly remember what it was, but anyway, he enlisted Lynn's help and carefully instructed her in how to feed the fire to keep a constant temperature. He then set off for town."

Lionel paused for a moment, took a sip of his drink and then continued. "Well, as Lynn explained it to me, she was a bit curious. At fourteen she was just about at the right age for curiosity. You have to remember that she had never tried moonshine, and as she tended the flame and watched the trickle of the clear liquid out of the condenser, she got this idea. She took a small enameled cup that was at hand, holding it under the trickle. She then tried a sip. I guess at first she gagged a little at the bite of the shine, but after a bit she decided it was not too bad. The end result, as you may have guessed, was that when Dad returned from his errand, he found Lynn fast asleep near the still. The fire was stone-cold."

All at the table chuckled at the story. Murdoch poured a new round and glanced at his watch. "Well, guys, I guess this will be the last one for me. Fifty years ago would be a different story, but I'm afraid I'm not as spry as I once was."

"Likewise for me," replied Mike. "It's early to bed and early to rise."

The setting sun had reached the water of the inlet, and a fiery reddish glow encompassed the western horizon. The last rays of sunlight entered the living room window and illuminated the whiskey bottle, which sat, now only one-third full, on the kitchen table, causing it to appear ruby red, the color of the rhubarb whence it had sprung. The arbutus tree stood in partial shadow, a shadow not quite as deep as that which enveloped the poplar tree so far away.

The light of a gigantic moon bathes the quiet land. All is quicksilver and shadow. A fitful breeze has sprung up from the south. A lone owl calls his soulful "whoo whoo" to the shadowed farmstead. The tired old house seems to sigh as the wind haunts the empty rooms, the window glass having long since vanished. The rhubarb patch stands in the shadow, invisible in the gloom.

Tomorrow the sun will rise again and the rhubarb will be revealed as it has been for a hundred years, since it was first planted by the original homesteader. It will stand proudly in the bright July sun as eternal as the prairie wind, as enduring as the ever-living sky. The surrounding meadow will be filled with

A Touch of Rhubarb

wildflowers, the air with the fragrance of the clover. The buzzing of the bees will soothe any passing listener. The call of a lonely meadowlark will be carried on the breeze, the same breeze that will flutter the leaves of the trees in the nearby poplar thicket. The rusting old grain binder will still be visible, half hidden in the thicket.

Will there be the sound of children playing, the rattle of trace chains and the snorting of horses as they switch their tails at the flies? Will you see the wood smoke from the chimney even on this hot summer day or smell the fragrance of fresh bread or a rhubarb pie baking in the oven? Will you feel the expectation of a great tomorrow when all things will be well? Will you sense a hush descending upon the meadow? The old house will stand mute but seem to whisper, "They came, they lived, they had hope and now they are no more." The wind will sing its mournful dirge, for no one will be there.

BURY ME IN CRABTREE

"Well, hello there, stranger. What's that you say? You'll have to speak up a bit. My hearing ain't what it used to be since I passed my eightieth birthday. Oh, you're asking what town this is? Well, I'm proud to say it's Crabtree, Saskatchewan. There used to be a sign just where the road comes into town, but it got knocked down in a windstorm a couple of years back. Ain't nobody got around to putting it up again. How the town got its name? Well, I had always been of a mind that it was named after that big old crab apple tree just back of the post office. No, not where the post office is now, at the general store, but at the old post office just past the corner, on your left. They closed that one down twenty-five years ago, but you can still see the old crab apple tree if you look just behind the building. It used to grow the sourest crab apples this side of anywhere, and I can certainly vouch for that. Strange name for a town? Not really, considering that when the crab tree had been planted, and I'm talking here about some years before my time, it was probably the only tree visible within sight. With this being the southern part of the province, there was pretty much only grass as far as you could see. Even now that there are more trees that have been planted by the townsfolk over the years, you will still be hard-pressed to see any at first glance.

"You're looking for the Elwood Smith farm? That'll be just west about a mile. No use going down there right now, though. Elwood will be out on his north half, working up his summer fallow, and his wife, Miz Smith, will be down to the school at Merton City, waiting to pick up the young 'uns after class. They usually come and go on the school bus, but today being Friday, I believe Miz Smith will be doing her weekly shopping, and she usually picks the kids up right after school. Gets them home about an hour before the bus would. We used to have a school here, but they decided that there weren't enough kids in this area so they moved them to the school at the next town. The Smiths should both be home in about three hours. Set yourself down on the bench over there. The afternoon will pass quickly enough. No, there's no coffee shop around. We used to have a café, but that burned down sixteen years ago. No one considered it worthwhile to rebuild.

"I often come out here to set on these warm spring afternoons, and I always pack a thermos flask of coffee. You're welcome to a cup. I just happen to have a spare cup here. There you go. Just hold the cup and I'll pour. I have to admit that it may not seem much by your standards, but, yes, it passes the time to set and watch the world go by. A quiet town, you say? I suppose it is, but it wasn't always like this. We used to have three elevators in the town, a railroad, several stores and cafés, a theater, a blacksmith shop, a hotel, a barber shop and even a bank, all mostly gone now. Some of the old buildings have been torn down, others burned and a few are still standing, abandoned and boarded up. Used to be almost five hundred people here at the peak. Now, if memory serves correctly, we number about sixty souls. I live on a ten-acre parcel just past the edge of town, there on the north side. Not much to keep me busy anymore. Oh I still put in my garden every spring, but once that's finished there ain't much else to do except pray for rain and watch the garden grow.

"I like to rest my bones here, right next to where the railroad station used to stand. These two benches are all that's left. People used to set on these benches, either waiting for a train to catch or just to watch the old steam engine roll into town on a Friday night. Everyone was always curious as to who was leaving, who was arriving and the like. Used to be teams and wagons and more than just a few automobiles lined up along the streets, everybody coming in for their weekly shopping and a visit with their neighbors. Stores always stayed open until late on Fridays. Time moves along, though. All things change, and not for the better. They tore up the rails almost twenty years ago. The station burned to the ground one night shortly after. Never did know what caused the fire. The elevators had already been closed down before, and they were tore down, one by one, and carted away for the lumber.

"Why didn't I leave here, go to the city, you say? I never could see any reason for it. There was always plenty of work for me here, hiring out to the local farmers. Wages weren't as great I suppose, but then it didn't cost much to get by. I went once to the city. People rushing around everywhere, everyone in a hurry to get nowhere. This was during the war when I was in an all-fired hurry to join up. Damn fool doctor said my ticker was bad. Well, I couldn't argue with him then, but I guess that whatever was the cause was cured by sixty years of hard work. I'm still here and expect to be for many more years to come. After that episode I was never so glad to get back. Ain't hardly left since. Why, I recall Ted Humphry, left here when he was about twenty-five years of age. Had some notion about making it big in the city. He came back to stay some twenty years later. Almost a stranger he was, coming into town in that long black Cadillac. Weren't many at the funeral when they laid him in the plot at the cemetery. The preacher who spoke over him hadn't ever known him.

"Married, you ask? No, never thought I could afford it. Never hankered much for kids of my own and, well, anything else that was required, there was always Miz Tilley. Who was she, you say? She was a lady who ran one of the local cafés some fifty or sixty years ago. Handsome woman, even in middle age

SHADOWS IN THE WIND

as I remember. She had been married to a no-account for some years. It was shameful how he treated her. Drinking all the time, coming home drunk and beating her on occasion, but all things come around and he broke his fool neck one night. Fell from his horse coming home from one of his sprees. No tears shed on his account. Everyone thought that Miz Tilley would be much better off without him around. She was, let me tell you. She opened up that café with the proceeds of the farm sale. For a number of years, time treated her right. She was still a fairly young woman at that time, and after her experience with marriage she swore that she would never make that mistake again, but she still had her needs, and although her business prospered during the week, every Saturday night the café would be shut at six o'clock. The goings-on behind the lace curtains upstairs would be whispered about, but I can tell you that many a young buck got his first taste of the bright lights without ever seeing the big city. Sometimes when more than one showed up, they would get to arguing and fighting, but not for long, I can tell you. Miz Tilley's word was law, and I swear she did more to preserve the peace and quiet of the community than all the constabulary in the district. I can say that I was one of them young bucks, but even now I'm shamed to speak this way of Miz Tilley because in the years that I knew her I never once heard her speak an unkind word of anyone, even that no-account husband of hers. Oh sure, some of the women did not approve of the way she lived her life, but most just let it lie. Only Miz Beechcroft, who owned the hotel at that time, with her husband, Roger, ever really made an issue of it. I still recall, though, that there were far fewer empty pews at the church at Miz Tilley's funeral than there was at Miz Beechcroft's.

"As you can see, there ain't many businesses left that are still open. There's the hotel and beer parlor, but I can't recall the last time they rented a room, and although the beer parlor gets busy

BURY ME IN CRABTREE

on Saturday afternoon, when the farmers from the area come in to sip a few or the occasional stranger pauses to quench his thirst, it usually stays very quiet during the week. I stop in there once in a while, but at my age, coffee is about as strong a drink as I can handle.

"Oh, do you mind if I light up? No, you don't? Thank you. I took to smoking a pipe some years back. Used to roll my own, but lately the arthritis in my hands has been getting the best of me. Wasted more tobacco trying to roll 'em than I got into the cigarette. Never did like those tailor-mades. Too expensive for one thing, and I always suspected that they didn't do you all that much good.

"Yes, that's the general store just down the street there. Oh, they sell some groceries and a few necessaries, handle the mail and even tried selling liquor for a spell. Not much call for that around these parts anymore. Most of the people left in town are past their drinking years. The church has been closed up for a few years as well, ever since the last preacher passed on to his reward. We all expected that another preacher would show up, but none ever did. On second thought, I guess most of the people here are past their sinning years too.

"If you'll look down the street, two doors past the old post office, about halfway along that next block, you can see that two-story building, the one that's all boarded up, with the sagging roof. That used to be our biggest general store. Been closed for almost thirty years, ever since we laid the owner, Sam Sloane, to his final rest. You had to know Sam to appreciate him. He'd been in the war for three years. Came back with a shot-up left arm. Never healed quite right. That arm was always a little bit stiff and he always made a show out of favoring it, but it surely didn't hold him back. You got to remember that, at the time, his store carried a lot of different stock including clothes, hardware, gro-

Shadows in the Wind

ceries, meat and even some farm implements as well. Well, sir, it was the sale of the meat where Sam got the most use of that arm. Whenever he placed a cut of meat on the scales, his left thumb would be resting, unseen, just on the edge of the scales. I swear that Sam's thumb sold for more per pound over the years than any prime side of beef there ever was. Mean, you say? Not really. Only those he knew could afford it would pay slightly more. Those in need could usually count on a helping hand from Sam. I recall that he carried Bob and Marie Thurlow on his books for eight months during a time of illness in their family, or another time when I stood at the back of the church and listened to the preacher say the last words over Lloyd Wright. Sam and his wife, Maude, were in the second pew. I could see the tears trickle down Sam's cheeks, and I knew that it wasn't because Lloyd had owed him seventy-eight dollars when he died. They had been hunting and fishing companions for years.

"Was a time when I wondered where everyone had got to. Many of the folk did move away over the years. There were many dry years, not too hospitable to farming. Also affected the businesses in town. They say that the grass is always greener in your neighbor's pasture. Maybe for some that was so. All I can say is that many left and never returned except for those that came back to rest in the cemetery yonder. You can't see it from here. It's about a quarter mile past the town limits, just to the west there, right along the old railroad grade. It's a pretty place. Except for the stone and wood markers, it looks like a stretch of prairie, covered with a clean blanket of snow in the winter and a fresh carpet of wildflowers in the spring. To me it always seemed sacrilegious to disturb the place with the digging of a new plot, but the land has a way of healing, and in no time at all the scars are gone. Yes, for many that left, the road was long indeed, longer than they had ever planned, but for others it was only that quarter of a mile and they stayed true to their roots forever.

"Oh, there goes Miz Jenkins, off to get her mail at the store, I suppose. Usually she stops to pass the time of day whenever she sees me sitting here enjoying the sun, but I guess she saw that I had company today, and she is a bit self-conscious. Her husband, Alfred, sure wasn't that way. He was our local barber for more years than I can remember. Gave a good haircut too, as I recall, but how he loved to talk. If business was slow, and it often was, he wouldn't let you out of the barber's chair for an hour and a half. A captive audience is hard to come by. Always kept a pot of coffee on the wood stove in the back room. Usually three or four guys setting there, drinking coffee and swapping lies, even if they weren't waiting for a haircut. Hasn't been a barbershop here since Alfred passed on. I get my hair cut at Miz Marley's house over at the end of the street. She just does it as a kind of favor for friends. Not the same, though, not the same anymore.

"What do I do to pass the time, you ask? Well, there is still a sort of ladies auxiliary here. They hold a weekly bingo at the old hall, and every once in a while there is a potluck supper. The old theater is still standing, over on that next corner there. If you look close in the front window, you can still see the poster of the last picture show that played there, and you know, that was thirty-five years ago. The blacksmith shop next door has been closed even longer. The place looks as if it was deserted only yesterday, except that everything, every tool and piece of equipment, is covered in dust. Other than that there is the television to watch, although I find it difficult to figure at times, with all the news of wars and such. Why do people get to fighting when there is so much more to a peaceful existence? That is one of the reasons I enjoy just setting here whenever the weather is fine. Just kind of let the seasons wash over me, take what I get and be grateful. You know, sometimes when I set here in the evening of a summer's day, just

SHADOWS IN THE WIND

when the twilight is falling, especially when the clouds are building in the east and the lightning is dancing just over the horizon, I look towards the east along the old railroad grade. I swear that I can see a faint glow off in the distance, like the headlight of an old steam engine. After a few moments it just disappears. I hope to be here for many years yet, but I sometimes like to think that when my time comes, that headlight will appear and it will just keep coming, growing in size as it approaches, the steam whistle sounding, carrying across the miles like it used to so many years ago, and it will pull up here where the station used to be. I will take a last look around, say my goodbyes and get on board for that final journey. Not far, mind you, only that last quarter mile. Yes, sir, you can bury me in Crabtree when my years are done.

"Now you can see one reason why I never left. If I had moved to that big city, I would have to spend eternity among strangers. Here in this place I can rest with friends. Oh sure, there were some petty differences, but you know, when I look back I surely realize there never was a finer bunch.

"Well, I guess the time has come for you to run along. The Smiths should be coming home soon. If you play your cards right, you'll be just in time for supper. I know that Miz Smith sets a mighty fine table. I've had the privilege of putting my feet under that table a time or two in recent years, and I can tell you that it was something to think of on a winter's night when I'd be having toast and cold beans for a quick supper. Remember me to Elwood and Miz Smith, and if you ever come by this way again and see me setting here, by all means stop and chew the fat a while. I always like to see a new face. Mind the potholes and watch for the big red barn on your right. You can't miss it. Goodbye and come again."

A CHRISTMAS MEMORY

"Childhood memories, how gently they linger in the mind," mused Elmer as he gazed across the barren fields covered by a light dusting of snow. For a moment his thoughts traveled backwards through the decades to his preschool years in the late 1940s. He had been the youngest of seven children growing up on a small farm on the prairies of Manitoba, and the borders of his world had been the barbwire fences that surrounded the quarter of land that was now in his sight. Although the buildings that had once stood here were long gone, he could still picture in his mind the many pleasant scenes of his early years. He wondered why he had taken so long to return.

As he opened the door of the shiny new Mercedes, now slightly dusty from the last few kilometers of gravel road, he felt, deep within his lungs, the crisp bite of the early November breeze as the last rays of a setting sun illuminated the landscape before him. The small town several kilometers ahead of him was his destination, but he had felt the need to pause here for a short while to collect his thoughts and, perhaps, remember a time when the unquenchable fire of youth still filled his being, and the world lay unspoiled for him to conquer. A half-dozen oak trees, mostly bare of leaves, stood near the shoulder of the road. Elmer shivered slightly as he watched an errant gust of wind pluck the single remaining leaf and swirl it through the air before allowing it to kiss the earth and rest in the final embrace of the coming winter.

Elmer felt the weight of sadness settle upon him when he realized that he was now alone. Arnold, the last of his siblings, would be laid to rest tomorrow in the small cemetery that lingered in a remote corner of Elmer's mind. After the passing of their parents some three decades before, the family had scattered across the country. None had remained here. Over the years they had succumbed, one by one, to the natural order of life's progress. One by one they passed through his mind. Charlie was the eldest, followed by Lucy, Mary, Raymond, Margaret and Arnold. Arnold, when he learned that he only had a few months to live, had returned to his hometown to finish out the final chapter of his life. Tomorrow he would join their parents in that peaceful place.

Remembering the time, about twenty-seven years earlier, when he had decided to leave the place of his birth, Elmer recalled that he had few qualms about his departure. Life was marching on. There were no ties upon him here. He would conquer the world and bend it to his will. The good life would be his. There would be no more want, no more need, all would be as he envisioned. Working for some years in the construction industry, he had used every opportunity to exercise his business acumen, eventually gaining ownership of not just one, but several business ventures. Oddly enough, the glamour of the boardrooms and the plush offices seemed rather unimportant at this moment. The years had slipped away. Money and power could not take the place of family. He realized, after all this time, that perhaps he had taken the wrong path.

As he continued his vigil, lost in his memories, his gaze passed over to the quarter of land immediately adjacent to his home quarter. He had no idea who lived there now, but as his eyes wandered across the landscape, a single object drew his attention, demanding he focus on it alone. Rising from the center of the cluster of oaks and poplars, towering over them by several meters and standing starkly against the ever-darkening sky, was a lone

A Christmas Memory

spruce tree, blunted on top and conspicuous, as it was the only evergreen in sight. A small smile appeared on Elmer's face as the evergreen tree conjured up a vision in his mind, a vision of a special Christmas from a time long ago.

As the details became clearer in his mind, Elmer recalled that the vision involved Charlie, his oldest brother, gone these past twenty years. Elmer visualized a time frame of a couple of years after the Second World War. Charlie had come of age and enlisted in 1944. He completed his training and went overseas just as the war was drawing to a close. After serving as a military policeman in England for a number of months, he had returned home. He was no longer the awkward farm boy he had been. He had traveled the world; he had "seen the elephant," so to speak, and he brought home with him not only his memories, but also a sense of humor. He had remained in this area for only a year or so before embarking on a career with the railroad. This entailed a move to a town a couple of hundred miles away. Charlie, as Elmer remembered, was the first to leave.

Turning slightly to lessen the effect of the gusting wind as his thoughts traveled back through the decades, Elmer recalled that, during his early years, the search for a Christmas tree was always a high point in the season. This usually involved a hike of many miles, sometimes in very cold temperatures. Evergreens were a rare commodity in this area. One sparkling, crisp December day, Charlie walked into the house with a fine specimen. The family quickly applied the meager decorations. Upon the very top of the tree, which seemed to Elmer, at four years of age, a towering edifice indeed, they carefully positioned a silver-colored star made of a foil material. In front of this star was a small candle, placed in a holder designed to catch the dripping wax and prevent the magnificent tree from catching fire. Surely a finer tree had never been.

Elmer could only wonder at the beauty of the tree, the flickering candle flame reflected from the many mismatched ornaments that seemed to glow with a fire of their own in the darkness of a December evening before the kerosene lamp was lit. He had never questioned the source of that tree, and only in later years did he find out where it had originated. The magic that tree exerted on a four-year-old mind, along with the efforts expended by his mother in the preparation of the Christmas feast and by his father in the creation of simple, handmade gifts, would never be forgotten.

Elmer remembered that, after her marriage, his older sister Lucy had settled with her husband, Adam, on the quarter section adjoining the home place. They had resided there for a number of years before deciding that a manufacturing job for Adam, and a move to the city, would be beneficial to their lifestyle. On their farm, very near the road, was the grove of poplar and oak trees. Hidden in the center of this wood was a single spruce tree, the only one on the quarter section. Charlie, with his well-developed sense of humor, decided that a hike in the frigid weather would hardly be worthwhile when opportunity knocked so handily at the door. Unbeknownst to anyone, he removed the top of the spruce tree, just enough for that wonderful Christmas tree. At that time the spruce was not as tall as the surrounding wood, and for several months nobody even noticed that a part of it was gone. Neither Lucy nor Adam ever did find out who the culprit was, and Elmer himself only learned the facts from Charlie in later years.

With a sense of loss, Elmer realized that more than fifty years had passed. Charlie and the Christmas tree were history, yet he thought about them still. The tree, with its blunted top, had almost faded into the increasing gloom, but to Elmer it seemed to say, accusingly, "Where is my crown?"

As he entered the warmth of the car's interior and prepared to drive those last lonely miles to the small town, Elmer won-

A Christmas Memory

dered if he would be willing to trade all he had to relive just once that Christmas of long ago, surrounded by the warmth of family and the comforting presence of that wonderful Christmas tree. He knew that it could never be.

As the car pulled away, the headlights cutting a swath through the gathering darkness, Elmer's eyes were drawn to the rearview mirror. Only a silhouette of the spruce tree was visible in reflection. As the automobile traveled forward, the stars in the sky seemed to move along the tree line. For a single moment, his wish was granted. The humble spruce tree and a star came into alignment. The light of memory shone brightly upon the tree's crown, shining like a beacon across the decades from a gentler time.

A LOONY TUNE or
A PRAIRIE MELODY

It was a golden kind of morning, not the kind of gold that you could spend, but one that you could enjoy, the gold of the mid-September autumn colors and the gold of the sunlight itself hinting at a wonderful, lazy day.

The car moved along at a sedate speed below the posted limit. Anybody watching it would tend to wonder if he or she had entered a time warp. The vehicle was a 1957 Ford retractable hardtop model, white with red sides, matching white fender skirts and a chrome-covered continental kit. From the radio came the voice of Gogi Grant singing the song "The Wayward Wind." No, this was not the 1950s. It was actually mid September of the year 2001, on a morning full of promise. The local radio station was hosting a program broadcasting tunes from the fifties and sixties.

Startled slightly as he was brought back to the present by the roar of a passing semi, Jack realized that this was no time for woolgathering. Although the road was not overly crowded, he knew that he should pay more attention to his driving. This was, in fact, difficult to do as his mind wandered the back roads of his memories. All of the passing farmsteads over these last few kilometers were familiar to him, not in their present form, but more in the way that he remembered them from forty years before when he had left this area of his youth, to take up residence in British Columbia. Returning now to his home in Vancouver after a visit with a friend in Ontario, he had decided, on a whim, to take a

SHADOWS IN THE WIND

detour through this area of Manitoba north of the Trans-Canada Highway that he still remembered so well. The small town of Winslow was an hour ahead. He would stop for an early lunch there, as it was just after 10:00 am.

Winslow had not changed a great deal in the last four decades in terms of population. Several newer buildings stood in the business section. Nestled among them was a smaller structure that Jack recognized as a restaurant from bygone years. The name on the overhead sign had changed, but the weather-beaten appearance of the place was the same as it had been forty years earlier. Looking around as he entered, Jack saw that the interior had been remodeled recently. The pictures in his mind recalled the high-backed booths that had existed way back when. These were gone and had been replaced with individual tables flanked by simple but sturdy chairs. This gave the place a more open appearance than he remembered. He took a seat near the window and was immediately brought a menu by a waitress, slim of build with dark hair and a friendly smile on her face.

"Good morning, sir," beamed the middle-aged woman. "Our special today is pork sausage and vegetables, soup or salad to start, at nine seventy-five."

Jack replied, "Thank you, I believe I will check the menu first." He remembered that same meal combination from decades before. It used to be priced at one dollar and sixty-five cents. He settled for a bowl of homemade soup and a sandwich. After finishing his meal and enjoying a leisurely second cup of coffee, he paid his bill and went outside.

Stepping into the warmth of the midday sun, Jack paused for a moment and looked lovingly at his car. He had first laid eyes on one of this type in Vancouver when he had arrived there at seventeen years of age. He vowed then, to himself, that he would have one, but it had taken almost four decades for the dream to come true. The price that he had paid just a short year before had been several times the original purchase price of the vehicle, but it was worth every penny. He liked to call it his time machine, and whenever he was behind the wheel he could imagine that he was a teenager once more. Elvis was still the king and the road of life stretched forever ahead.

Luxuriating in the feel of the soft leather upholstery, Jack followed the road out of Winslow heading in a westerly direction. Twenty minutes later he was passing by an old farm site. There was a large, older house surrounded on three sides by a grove of evergreen trees. This was followed by a scattering of meadows bordered by thickets of willows and stands of oak trees.

Jack remembered this home site. It was called the Macdonald pony ranch. He had not known the owner personally, but he remembered that he had a passion for collecting old farm equipment and automobiles. Jack could not remember if there had ever been any ponies here, but he recalled the many acres covered with rusting steam tractors, gasoline and diesel tractors, binders, threshing machines, cars and trucks along with every other piece of farm memorabilia that could be amassed over a period of five decades or more. Most were gone now, leaving behind empty patches of meadow covered only with a multicolored blanket of weeds and grasses. The old man had passed on a few years back, and the pieces of his collection had departed as well, to collectors in all corners of the country, leaving only the occasional rusted hulk to mark a lifetime of dedication.

The traffic ahead of Jack began to slow, and he touched his brakes as he saw a sign on the shoulder of the road.

Accident Scene Ahead

Very shortly the traffic came to a stop and Jack craned his neck, trying to see the obstruction that was several hundred meters

SHADOWS IN THE WIND

ahead. After about ten minutes a young woman approached his car. She wore a hard hat and the brightly colored vest of a traffic-control person.

"There has been an accident between a semitrailer and a car at the highway intersection ahead. The truck has rolled and spilled its load of lumber. The police are at the scene and the ambulance will be arriving shortly. The highway will probably be closed for a couple of hours. Sorry for the inconvenience, but it will take a while to clean up the mess."

Jack thanked her for the information and settled back in his seat. The rising wail of the approaching ambulance sounded in his ears as it sped by in the left-hand lane. He thought that he would walk along the shoulder of the road to a place near the accident scene to view the situation firsthand. Closing the car door behind him, he did not lock it. He would only be gone for a few minutes.

Approaching the scene, Jack could see that the entire roadway was buried under spilled lumber. The tractor unit lay on its side in one ditch, while the small car, which had been hit by the truck on its right side, lay in the other ditch. It appeared to Jack that the car had turned left onto the highway from the right, cutting off the truck driver and causing him to swerve. As the ambulance crew and the two policemen worked diligently to extract the occupants from the vehicles, Jack could see that only the two respective drivers were involved. There were no passengers in either vehicle. Both drivers were conscious and able to converse with their rescuers. Neither appeared to be injured too severely, but the driver of the car could consider himself very lucky as his vehicle was only a meter or so from being buried by the load of lumber.

Jack returned to his car. He knew that it would be at least a couple of hours before the highway could be cleared. He was

A LOONY TUNE OR A PRAIRIE MELODY

faced with a choice. He could either backtrack, and try to make his way around the accident scene by way of the grid roads, or he could just relax and wait for the roadway to reopen. As he settled back into the car seat with the windows open and the sunshine warm on his skin, he decided that perhaps he would just doze here for an hour or so. His schedule was not pressed, and he had not slept well the night before.

Jack let his eyes wander as he sat there in a half stupor. He could see that he was sitting immediately adjacent to a small group of oak trees that were off to one side of the road. The oak trees were wearing the colors of fall, and sheltered within the trees was a quartet of ancient threshing machines. Three were grouped together. One of these was a larger Woods Brothers threshing machine, flanked by a Massy-Harris on one side and a Case machine on the other side. A few meters away was a smaller machine. Jack could not make out the manufacturer's name as it was obscured by a large patch of rust. These machines seemed to him not unlike a group of matriarchs, three of which were clustered together in a conspiratorial manner, while the one off by itself appeared to be dejected and forlorn, with one wheel missing and various other components gone. Fifty meters away, set in a willow thicket, was an old steam tractor. It looked to have been there a number of years. The front wheels had sunk into the earth to a quarter of their height, the massive chains on the steering mechanism lay broken on the ground, and the old boiler showed signs of a rupture at some time in the distant past.

For a moment Jack pondered how he assigned gender to these machines. The old tractor was no doubt male, supplying the brute strength for any job at hand, while the threshing machines were much like the pioneer women of the west, working alongside their men and birthing the uncounted bushels of grain that had been the lifeblood of the prairie for a hundred years. With only semi-conscious thought, he assigned names to the four machines: Mrs. Woods, Mrs. Harris, Mrs. Case and, as the name on the last thresher was unreadable, Mrs. Smith.

As he settled back, his eyes becoming heavy, Jack realized that a lively breeze had sprung up in the meadow. It had found some bit of piping on one of the threshing machines and was playing a tune, something of a loony tune, a tune played upon the prairie in the middle of a warm September day. A dust devil twirled its way across the meadow, and the elusive fragrance of a far-off burning stubble field invoked pleasant recollections in Jack's memory. As he slowly drifted away, the thought passed through his mind, "If these threshing machines could talk, what stories they could tell. What fascinating memories they would have. Yes, if only they could talk …"

"Well, did you ever see such nerve!" exclaimed Mrs. Woods. "Pulling out in front of the big fellow, cutting him off like that without even an if you please."

"What else would you expect from an automobile? I've always said that they were the worst riffraff you could ever see, doing nothing but driving around all day, never doing a lick of work," replied Mrs. Harris. "I was never in favor of them allowing all those cars to retire here to the same place as us working folk. I was ever so glad when they finally hauled them away, hopefully to that big foundry in the sky."

"Yes," Mrs. Case joined in, "that was certainly a red-letter day. Why, look out there on the highway. See that hussy decked out like a strumpet in all that red and white, with the fancy chrome and the leather upholstery. You can see that she certainly doesn't have to put too much effort into her existence. Imagine, almost fifty years old and still dressing like a teenager. Why, if my arthritis was not so bad, I think that I would go over there and rip her headlights out."

A Loony Tune or A Prairie Melody

Mrs. Smith remained as she had been, passive and unresponsive, uttering not a word.

Glancing at the old steam tractor in the willows a short distance away, Mrs. Woods continued, "I remember, in my day, that we certainly knew the value of a good day's work. My Willy and I would set heads to turning every time we moved across the countryside. Whimsical Willy, the master used to call him, because at times he would take a notion to balk at his tasks and could not always be depended on to perform as the master intended. He doesn't look like much now, sitting there in the willows. Ever since he got his hernia he just dozes away the seasons. You should have seen him in his younger days, proud as a peacock as we paraded from farm to farm, flexing those muscles as we threshed the crops, the black smoke belching from the stack, and the whistle ... Yes the whistle could be heard for miles in the golden September air. Now we are old. No one has much use for us anymore, but with a little tlc and perhaps a little grease and oil we could still show them how it's done."

"I too remember those days," answered Mrs. Harris. "It seems like only yesterday when the annual harvest was more of a celebration than a monotonous chore. Farm families would get together and share the workload as well as the equipment. Harvest time was usually a glorious time of year, especially if the crops were heavy. I still recall that, although the work was difficult, it was also satisfying. Even the coffee breaks in the field were like a festive occasion. It was at these times when the master would come around with the grease gun to ease my aching joints and to make those necessary adjustments that were guaranteed to restore my vigor and allow me to attack the job at hand with a renewed intensity. How I wish sometimes that I was fifty years younger with still a reason to exist."

After a short pause, Mrs. Case sighed as she continued, "I certainly believe that we should be proud of our accomplishments. I recall the thirties. There was not much crop to thresh in those times, but one memory that lingers in my mind is of a stolen moment shared by a young field hand and a farmer's daughter, beneath a gigantic full moon, on a blanket laid upon a fresh bed of straw that, of course, was provided by me. From this moment began a dynasty. I have been told that the descendants now number more than a hundred, and some of them collectively own more than a township of land just a few miles to the east of here. Others of the family have moved to the various city regions, spread from sea to sea. Most of them, I hear, have been highly successful and have done their share to drive the wheels of industry and enhance the halls of commerce. It gives me a warm feeling to know that I played a small part in it all."

A peaceful moment descended upon the meadow. The errant breeze continued to play its tune upon the pipes, slightly more sedate now, perhaps less a loony tune and more a melody, a prairie melody, played upon a warm September afternoon. The oak leaves fluttered in time to the music, and the lone maple tree blushed redly at the goings-on. Whimsical Willy slumbered on in the willows, oblivious to it all.

The voice of Mrs. Woods intruded upon the late summer scene as she turned her attention to the outsider in the group, Mrs. Smith. "Dearie, why are you always so quiet? You are of a similar age to the rest of us. You have traveled the roads and byways, and I am sure that you have memories that you would like to share."

The seconds ticked by and a shudder seemed to pass through the old threshing machine standing apart from the rest. With a sob, Mrs. Smith began. "You are very lucky to have had such wonderful times. I wish that I could remember my younger years as fondly as you. The thirties were a difficult time. Mr. Rumley

A Loony Tune or A Prairie Melody

and I traveled the area, threshing what crops there were, but many times we stayed idle because the drought and the heat had done their work too well. Our master at that time did not treat us well. Many times we labored without the benefit of adequate grease and oil. My belting was in a terrible state. Mr. Rumley was getting along in years, but we did the best we could. There was a young man who had worked in the threshing crew for several seasons. Many a time, I noticed that he looked longingly at me with a wistful expression on his face.

"One autumn day the master decided that he could not continue with the farming operation any more. A deal was struck and the young man purchased Mr. Rumley and me from him. The next couple of years were much improved. We received regular maintenance from our new master and, if I remember correctly, I had never felt so well before. Unfortunately the good times came to an end. It was about midway through the war. The crops had improved somewhat, and we were untouched by the carnage that was going on in the European theater. Why, I still recall hearing of the tremendous number of casualties among the machines sent over there to fight, but we carried on, seemingly spared those trials and tribulations, little knowing that the end was near.

"It was a day in September, very much like today. Mr. Rumley and I had finished the season and we were coming home. The master was driving and I followed behind, tired but very content at having completed the yearly task so well. We had just entered the home yard and were proceeding to our rest area to one side of the barn. The master's young wife stood in the yard waving as he drove by. Their three-year-old daughter stood holding her mother's hand. I remember her still. She was a beautiful child with hair the color of the ripened grain and eyes that would rival the bluest August sky. To her parents she was the light of their lives. Then it happened. As we passed the house, the little girl *broke free of her mother's grasp and darted forward.*

"'Daddy, Daddy, wait for me,' she cried. Then she tripped. I tried to avoid it. I really tried, but she fell beneath my wheel. I will never forget the sight of that child lying so still. The life seemed to go out of both her parents, and they could stay no more. In the winter of that year they moved in to the town. He joined the army and was eventually sent to join the war effort. He never returned, and she died the following autumn, of a broken heart no doubt.

"It was all my fault. If I hadn't been so clumsy I could have avoided the accident. Mr. Rumley was never quite the same either. He moped about for months until they finally came and hauled him away. I stayed on at the farm, alone, for years, weathering the winter snows, the violent thunderstorms and that eternal prairie wind until they finally sent me to this rest home. My wheel, the very wheel that did the damage, was removed, no doubt as punishment, and I was glad to see it go. I could no longer bear the sight of it. Here I have remained. It is not the elements that cause me to rust so. It is the tears, the everlasting tears. They never stop."

Silence returned to the meadow once more. All were speechless.

"Wake up, sir, wake up. The highway will be open in a few minutes."

Jack roused himself from his slumber. Bewildered, he looked around as he tried to reorient himself to his surroundings. "What a crazy dream," he thought as he gathered his wits about him.

The meadow was quiet. The only activity evident in the waning afternoon was that of the insects drawn out by the warm, late summer weather. The odd piping had ceased as the breeze had died.

The traffic-control person signaled the vehicles to move forward. Jack put his car into gear. As he pulled away, he glanced once more at the tableau beneath the oak trees. All seemed to be at rest. He spied a glimmer on the rusty area of the fourth threshing machine, sparkling like a diamond or perhaps some moisture reflecting in the sun, moisture in the afternoon of a cloudless September day, almost like tears.

"Nah!" he thought. "I've stayed too long. I'm beginning to hallucinate." He stepped on the accelerator and drove quickly away.

A tear trickled down the cheek of Mrs. Smith as she gazed into the distance.

NIGHT PASSAGE

Mile Zero. It had been a long time since Ray had thought of it. He leaned on his cane as he watched the idling engine that would carry him on his journey. His mind did not behold the modern diesel locomotive but rather that great black behemoth that he remembered from his younger days. With a sigh he slowly boarded the train and settled himself wearily into the upholstered seat of the day-coach, placed his cane carefully against the wall of the railcar by the empty window seat and waited for the almost imperceptible lurch of the train to let him know that they were under way.

It was August 15, 2003, and he was making this journey from The Pas, Manitoba, to Churchill, the onetime port city of the prairie, to touch base with his past, a past from which he had been absent for thirty-five years. He had flown into The Pas airport, via Winnipeg, from the west coast and would make the rest of this journey by train. The sun was high above the horizon and bathed the land in its golden light. The train began to move, and slowly the outskirts of the town slid away to make room for the forested vistas of the North Country. In just a few minutes the conductor, a young man by Ray's way of thinking, came by to collect the tickets. The journey was underway.

Ray Stiles, slight and graying, stooped over a bit as a result of an automobile accident three years earlier that had nearly cost him his life, took a mental inventory of the events that had led him here. It was the passing of his wife four years ago that had made him realize how quickly the years had flown. He had made plans

SHADOWS IN THE WIND

for this journey very soon after, but the accident had forced a lengthy convalescence and had left him with a pronounced limp.

He had spent the first thirty-nine years of his life in this North Country, and he knew it very well from Mile Zero, at The Pas, to the end of the line, where the rails of steel reached the waters of Hudson Bay. Why had he waited so long to return? He had moved his family to the western region of this vast land those many years before in search of a better life. With only a couple of trips back to this area over the intervening years, the decades had quickly fled, leaving him with a desire to revisit his past, a time that seemed like only yesterday. He knew that most of the people he remembered from those long-ago years had since departed, but at least one old friend, Wally Franklin, still lived in Churchill, and a visit with him was the purpose of this journey.

Wally, at seventy-nine years of age, had been a railroad engineer, and Ray, as a brakeman for the railroad, had worked with him for many years. Why Wally had chosen to remain in this isolated outpost in his retirement years was a mystery to Ray, but as Wally himself had said, he had no immediate family, and as long as the fellows in the white coats did not get him, he'd be okay. This was a private joke. The fellows in the white coats were just Wally's way of referring to the ever-present polar bears that migrated through the area. His was a life of simple pleasures. Wally and Ray had kept in touch sporadically over the years, and only a week earlier they had talked on the telephone. Ray was looking forward to the visit.

The shriek of the train whistle jarred Ray out of his reminiscing, and he looked through the glass at the passing scenes of evergreen forest, swamps and lakes. The names of the whistle-stop settlements drifted through his mind, Wekusko, Ponton, Wabowden, Lyddal, Earchman, Thicket Portage. Some still showed a scattering of run-down dwellings, while others had dis-

NIGHT PASSAGE

appeared from the scene, leaving only lingering memories of a different life, a time from long ago. The swaying of the passenger car betrayed the lack of maintenance on the rail bed in recent years, although, due to the advent of ribbon rail, the clickety-clack of the train wheels on the rail joints was absent. Quickly the miles drifted away.

The balance of the day passed uneventfully. Ray felt a pang of hunger and realized that he should eat his supper before the dining car shut down for the night at 8:00 pm. Retrieving his cane, he made his way back through the second day-coach, noticing that there were few passengers aboard on this summer evening. The sleeper cars were beyond the dining car, with the baggage car forward of the two day-coaches. Ray had not bothered with sleeping accommodations. The injuries from the auto accident left him unable to complete a whole night in a prone position, and he usually spent a part of his night snoozing in his recliner, which would be no different than passing the night in his seat in the day-coach. Lowering himself carefully into the dining car chair, he awaited the approach of the waiter.

"Good evening, sir," said the waiter in a cheery tone as he laid the menu down on the tabletop. "What can I get for you today?"

Ray glanced at the menu for a moment and ordered. "I'll just have a hot beef sandwich, coffee to start."

"Thank you," replied the waiter, writing on his notepad and quickly moving away to the next table as he made his way back to the kitchen area.

Ray gazed out the window of the dining car while he waited for his supper to arrive. The passing vistas were as he remembered from decades before. It was as though time had stood still, with only the aches in his body reminding him of the passage of the years.

The meal arrived and Ray ate slowly, savoring a last cup of

coffee before paying his tab and returning to the day-coach.

Absorbed in his memories, Ray paid no particular attention to the passing of the miles, although he did notice that he shared this day-coach with only four other people, two men sitting in separate seats and a couple — probably man and wife, he thought — sharing a seat at the rear of the coach. He suddenly realized that the train would soon be arriving in Pikwitonei, his hometown. This had also been his headquarters during the years he had spent working for the railway. They would only be stopping for half an hour, and although he planned on staying over for a couple of days, it would be on his return journey from Churchill. The town itself had shrunk dramatically over the years, and old acquaintances would be few. He would take that opportunity to visit the cemetery for a quiet farewell to the ones left behind.

The whistle of the engine signaled the departure of the train from Pikwitonei. The sun had passed beyond the horizon, and the land donned a cloak of shadow while the western sky was ablaze with the purple afterglow of an August evening on the northern prairie. Ray's mind recaptured lost memories, many of which had eluded him for years. About two and a half hours quickly passed after their departure from Pikwitonei. The town of Gillam came and went with only a short stopover, and he realized that they would soon be passing a certain small railroad siding. This triggered a significant recollection. There used to be a section house and a few scattered dwellings there some half a century before, but they would probably be gone. The train would pass by unnoticed in the dark. He would not see, but he would certainly remember.

The event he remembered had happened about 1952 if memory served correctly. Wally Franklin was the engineer, Dennis Warren was the conductor, Alan Senechal was the head-end brakeman, Albert Jones was the fireman and Ray himself had been the tail-end brakeman. Thinking back, Ray recalled, with a pang of sadness, that Dennis had been killed in a wreck beyond Gillam, about 1961 or so. Dennis had been a giant of a man, standing six foot six in his stocking feet. Ray had once seen him place a forty-five gallon drum of gasoline onto a flat car. Ray did not know what became of Alan, as he had left the employ of the railroad even before Ray did. Albert had completed his employment with the railroad and had retired in The Pas only to lose a valiant battle with cancer a couple of years later. The events of that night in mid-August 1952 came back as clearly as though they had happened yesterday.

The long, drawn-out wail of the steam engine echoed across the small town of The Pas as Wally Franklin advanced the throttle of the steam engine with one hand while pulling on the whistle cord with the other. Striking a confident pose, he sat at the controls of the steam engine with his ever-present, although often unlit, pipe in his mouth. He was a little on the stocky side, and with his freshly laundered overalls, matching railroad cap and walrus moustache he looked very much in charge of the great iron beast as he fixed his gaze firmly on the tracks ahead. Over the years he had perfected a steam train whistle with a personal signature, a slight inflection to the last note. Anyone along the right-of-way knew when Wally Franklin was at the controls.

This August afternoon in 1952 was overcast, with a heavier buildup of clouds to the northeast. The weather had been fairly hot over the last few days, and there would, no doubt, be a thunderstorm before dark. Brooding was perhaps the word to describe the weather. It did not bode well for a pleasant night.

Dennis Warren made his way through the day-coaches, collecting tickets and dispensing answers to the occasional desultory question ventured by a passenger. He nodded briefly to the newsie, who had already opened his stand, ready to dispense bits of comfort to the traveling public. The passenger load was quite high this evening. The Churchill traffic was fairly heavy these days, what with the American and Canadian armed forces activity at the port city. Also present were a good number of the local natives, most of whom would depart the train at their respective whistle-stops along the north line. Dennis knew it would be a busy night.

Albert Jones watched the flame critically as he placed another shovel full of high-grade coal upon the fire. He had been with the railroad for a couple of years and he had learned, through experience, that firing a locomotive was an art. It wasn't just a matter of throwing fuel in the fire and hoping it would burn. Each shovelful had to be carefully placed to ensure the fire burned with a clean flame and with proper ventilation to produce a maximum head of steam. Glancing at the gauge, he deposited one more load, then stood back and wiped the sweat from his brow. Taking a pack of cigarettes from his overall pocket, he shook one loose, placed it in his mouth and lit up. Dragging deeply on the cigarette, he idly scanned the passing countryside. He knew it would be a long shift, but he was up to it. He had done it many times before.

Alan Senechal and Ray Stiles worked their respective sections of the passenger train, each checking that everything was as it should be with the running gear. Every half hour or so, they could be seen on their rounds.

The cloud cover had been building. The sky, now dark with no sign of the evening afterglow, was lit up occasionally by a flash of lightning. This was immediately followed by the surly echo of thunder across the lonely land.

The journey continued without a hitch, with passengers disembarking or boarding at the various stops along the way.

Pikwitonei had arrived and departed, and eventually the town of Gillam was reached. Alan Senechal swung down from the steam engine as the train slowed to a stop. Removing his switch key from his pocket, he unlocked the padlock and threw the switch, allowing the passenger train to move into the siding. The train proceeded along the rails until the tail end was within the siding. On a lamp signal from Ray Stiles, the engineer brought the train to a halt once more while Ray realigned the switch for the main track. They would stay here for a short time to await the arrival of a through freight from Churchill, a train of empty grain cars heading back south for a refill. Dennis, the conductor, holding a clipboard with a sheaf of papers under his arm and with a rain jacket draped loosely over his shoulders, walked into the station. In very few minutes the thunder of the freight train beat upon the eardrums, and the smell of coal smoke became even more prevalent throughout the night. The freight train passed, the clickety-clack of its wheels exaggerated by the thumping of a flat wheel on one of the grain cars. It vanished, finally, into the gloomy darkness, leaving only the hiss of steam from the resting passenger train engine to be heard.

"All aboard," came the call as the passenger train prepared to continue on its way. The sound of the steam whistle was eclipsed by a flash of lightning, followed instantaneously by a roll of thunder. The silhouette of the moving train was highlighted momentarily against the shadowed backdrop of the seemingly endless forest, but there was no one there to see.

Ray was making his periodic inspection tour, checking all lighting and operating systems of the train. He had just emerged from the baggage car and entered the day-coach. Dennis was sitting in his customary seat in the railcar, perusing a stack of papers on his clipboard. He motioned to Ray as he walked by.

"I received orders from the dispatcher to pick up cargo at

the first siding beyond Gillam — a body, to be exact. We are to meet Constable Granger of the rcmp. He will load the body, and we have to deliver it to the coroner at Churchill."

Ray merely nodded. Although this was not a normal part of their schedule, it was certainly not unheard-of. He continued on his rounds, glancing out the window momentarily at the lightning dancing on the horizon, illuminating the glare of water as the train thundered on.

With the squeal of metal on metal as the air brakes were applied, the passenger train slowed to a stop. Their scheduled stop was at hand. Alan Senechal spotted the baggage cart next to a small shed located adjacent to the rails. A couple of lanterns cast their feeble light upon the trackside shed. Shadowy figures could be seen milling about. Farther from the track stood the section house with the light of a kerosene lamp illuminating only one window.

Dennis Warren stood back from the door of the baggage car while Ray Stiles slid open the door.

"Evening, men," said the young man who stepped into the car. "I'm Constable Granger." He quickly drew the conductor aside and proceeded to discuss the details of this night's work.

Ray Stiles looked into the gloom of the rain-soaked night and saw four silent figures standing in the shelter of the overhang of the shed roof. Beside them was a long wooden box. With his hand he motioned them forward, and they bent to grasp their burden, quickly placing it on the floor of the baggage car. He saw that they were native men, locals no doubt, all likely acquainted with the deceased. They moved the box to the place he directed and filed out the door, all but one. The fourth man looked for a few moments at the rough wooden box. He removed his hat in silent respect and then followed his companions into the darkened night.

Ray noticed that the box had no lid. Examining it more closely, he saw the figure of a native male, about forty years of age, who looked, for all the world, as though he were asleep. Turning to the conductor for further instructions, Ray saw that Constable Granger had finished his discussion and was leaving the baggage car. Dennis merely motioned for Ray to close the door and they were soon on their way once more.

Ray Stiles made his way forward, through the throng of passengers, most of them sleeping, in the second day-coach. When he had looked at his pocket watch just a few minutes before, he had seen it was 3:25 am, time for his round of inspection. Glancing out the window he saw a three-quarter moon suspended in the night sky. At least the storm had moved on.

Threading his way carefully around the occasional protruding leg or arm of a comatose passenger, he passed through into the lead day-coach area. He saw Dennis Warren in a rear-facing seat, arms folded, nodding a bit, succumbing to the boredom of the moment. Stopping to adjust a lamp at the forward end of the coach, Ray opened the door of the car and stepped into the passage between the lead coach and the baggage car. Immediately he was struck by the increased level of noise as the rattle and rumble of the running gear carried up through the metal floor of the passage.

Closing the door of the day-coach, he turned to open the door to the baggage car. With a start he realized that the door was opening of its own volition. Ray stood transfixed as the door swung fully open. There should have been no one in the baggage car, but someone was coming out. A lone figure emerged, shadowed by the limited light in the passage. A native man, Ray thought, based on the quick glimpse he got of the stranger as he stumbled by and entered the day-coach, closing the door behind him. Recovering from his discomfiture, Ray quickly entered the baggage car. He knew that figure. But it could not be.

Striding over to where the wooden box lay on the baggage car floor, he looked inside. It was empty.

Retracing his steps to the first day-coach, Ray scanned the seats quickly. The figure he sought was seated halfway along, gazing out the window into the night, a bewildered expression on his face.

Ray walked slowly by to where Dennis Warren sat, still trying to fend off the call of drowsiness. Leaning over so he could speak in a low tone he said, "Dennis, do you remember that fellow we picked up this side of Gillam?"

Dennis looked up at him, puzzled. "Yes, I do. What about him?"

"He's sitting three seats behind you."

Dennis looked at Ray for a few moments as though he thought that Ray had lost his senses. Then he sat upright and looked back to where Ray was subtly motioning. For a few moments neither one said a word; then Dennis arose, and both men walked to the seat where the lone figure sat.

"Excuse me," began Dennis as he attempted to initiate conversation with the man who sat staring out the window. Slowly the man turned his head, still looking bewildered and uncomprehending.

Ray, watching, realized that this fellow might not have too good a grasp of the English language. Quite often these people lived their entire lives in the forested North Country and spoke only their native tongue, Cree. Ray, on the other hand, having been raised in this area, had developed a good knowledge of the Cree language. He tapped Dennis on the shoulder. "Wait up a second, Dennis. Let me try."

Night Passage

Conversing in the Cree tongue, Ray finally saw the dawning light of comprehension begin to glow in the man's eyes. In reply to Ray's questions, he said that he had no idea what he was doing on this train. His last memory was coming into his cabin with a day's catch of fish. Beyond that he could remember nothing.

After assuring the man that everything was under control, Ray told him to just sit in his seat until they reached Churchill. He would then be taken to the hospital, where the doctor could examine him.

As though awakening from a dream, Ray's mind returned to the present. The scene of that fateful journey was replaced by the flash of lightning in the forest outside the window. A storm had developed while he was lost in memory. Ray realized that he was sleepy. Perhaps he could doze now, if just for a little while. He leaned back and closed his eyes, but still the thoughts would not go away.

He recalled the aftermath of that night from more than half a century ago. Dennis had telegraphed the agent at Churchill from some whistle-stop that Ray could no longer remember. An ambulance had been waiting at the station in Churchill upon their arrival, along with a member of the local rcmp. Their passenger had been dispatched to the hospital, and everything had returned to normal. About a week later, Ray recalled, he had seen the native gentleman again, this time when he boarded the train on a return journey to The Pas. He departed the train at the same place where they had picked him up just days before, choosing to spend the few hours of that trip in solitude, speaking to no one. Ray would have loved to question him, but he did not want to intrude. He had never seen the man again, yet from time to time he would wonder "Why?" A veil of darkness crept across Ray's mind.

A crash of thunder broke the grip of deep slumber and Ray struggled to regain his wits, for a moment wondering where he was. The storm was raging outside the speeding train, but inside the lights were dim. Looking about him, Ray saw that his fellow passengers had departed somewhere along the miles. He was alone.

Dimly he became aware of the *clickety-clack, clickety-clack* of the wheels. A heavy pall of something that looked and smelled like coal smoke swept by the coach windows, visible in the reflected light of a lightning flash. The long drawn-out wail of the locomotive called into the night. "Funny," thought Ray. "That sounded so much like Wally Franklin's signature whistle from so many years before." He felt a cool breath of air upon his face, as though somebody had opened the door that faced the baggage car. He looked quickly to the forward end of the coach. No one was there. He tried to rise from his seat but his limbs would not respond. His comprehension faded and the interior of the coach went dark.

Outside, in the storm, the dark engine thundered on, the long drawn-out wail carrying across the marshland, a long yellow beam from the single headlamp boring into the night.

Ray felt a hand gently shaking his shoulder as he struggled from the depths of sleep. He looked up to see the young conductor.

"Churchill in one hour, The Factor's Table restaurant will be open at 6:00 am for breakfast. It's only half a block from the station."

Ray thanked the man and turned to look out the window at the passing scenery of stunted trees and wetlands. He knew that they were not far from the tundra. Reflecting on the memory of the last hour he thought, "It was all a dream."

Night Passage

Ray retrieved his suitcase and deposited it in a coin-operated locker at the station. He then made the short walk to the restaurant. He would have his breakfast and then he would think about calling Wally. Ray knew that Wally had, in recent years, moved into an apartment. He would ask for directions at the restaurant.

Entering the café, Ray saw that only two people were present, a middle-aged waitress and a tired-looking ambulance attendant. Neither appeared too cheerful, and they were engaged in earnest conversation. A battered old ambulance was parked outside.

The waitress had taken Ray's order and was just turning away when he asked about Wally. "I'm looking for directions to the place of a friend of mine. Ice fields Manor is the name of the building. Wally Franklin is my friend's name."

The waitress stopped suddenly and exchanged a worried look with the ambulance attendant. Slowly the attendant looked in Ray's direction and began to speak. "Wally Franklin died last night. We actually got the call at about three thirty this morning. He was having chest pains but managed to use the telephone. There was nothing we could do. He was gone before we reached the medical center. I'm sorry."

Ray sat stricken. From somewhere far across the tundra, or perhaps only in his own mind, came again the long drawn-out wail of a steam engine with that peculiar note at the end.

JACK'S JOURNEY

"Ah, it's good to be going home," thought Jack as he settled himself down on the passenger seat of the beat-up red Ford pickup. His buddy, Jerry Wiesmueller, sat behind the wheel, somber-looking at forty years of age, with a slight paunch showing above the large silver belt buckle and his black hat pulled down in front to shade his eyes from the rising sun.

Looking to the right and left before pulling out onto the highway, Jerry "harrumphed" as he cleared his throat, depressing the accelerator with a tooled leather boot and merging with the traffic on the busy road. Unobtrusively he wiped a single tear from the corner of his eye. Manitoba was two days away. He might as well get this show on the road.

Jack knew that Jerry would not be in a mood for talk, and, slouched down on the seat as he was, there was not too much view of the passing countryside, but he had been there before, knew it by heart. He would see it all in his mind, as it had been before he left his prairie home to follow the great unknown some twenty years earlier. He had only been back to the home place a few times since, but he had covered all of the country between, as well as much of the western U.S. of A., in the course of his thirty-eight years of life, much of it on the rodeo circuit. It would be great to see home again, maybe recall some of the old memories of his boyhood years.

"John Emerson Slade," thought Jack as he sat in the truck. How he had hated that name. The "Emerson" moniker had been hung on him by his mother, Myrna, who had been a campus queen at an eastern university in the very late fifties before somehow becoming entangled with Walter Slade, Jack's father, through some chance encounter that Jack could not now recall having heard the details of. Her passion had been poetry, and Ralph Waldo Emerson was a favorite of hers. From university campus to a Manitoba grain farm was quite a change for her, but that was where John had been born and where he had spent his younger years. "Jack E. Slade" was how he signed his cheques. He had often thought that he had disappointed his mother with his attitude toward so-called higher learning. "Emerson" he would not admit to. His thoughts drifted as the miles sped away.

A lazy August breeze ruffled ten-year-old John's hair as he sat on his perch in the tree house. Although it was only a rickety platform made of leftover boards of varying width and thickness, with a sloping canvas roof to keep out most of a passing shower, to John it was a castle of dreams. He had built it with his own two hands, although, if the truth were known, his father had supervised, discreetly adding a bit of help when young John's youthful exuberance carried him in the wrong direction. The oak trees upon which the tree house sat had grown close together, a trio set in a triangle on a slight rise of land, just begging for a construction project of this sort.

John looked out across the fields stretching to the distant horizon in the afternoon haze, many showing the color of the ripening grain swaying in the warm, west wind, with only an occasional towering white cloud passing overhead. John was watching, but he saw none of this. He was watching the three horses in the neighbor's pasture as they frolicked in the midsummer afternoon. He admired the rippling muscles of the animals as they cavorted with abandon, especially when they sensed a coming storm. He was a kindred spirit to these horses. He would love to run with them, to feel the rush of the wind upon his skin and experience the power of the untamed. John knew that his father had been an ardent rodeo rider in his youthful days, but a badly broken leg had left him with a permanent limp and a realization that he would now lead the life of a Manitoba farmer. Although John had tried with all his might, he could not convince his father to buy him a pony.

The sound of the tape deck awakened Jack from his reverie. He wished that Jerry had picked something else to play. The duo playing was not a favorite of his. No point in saying anything, though. Jerry had always been hardheaded and would usually go his own way. Jack's thoughts turned inwards once more as the low, timbered hills of British Columbia's Cariboo region swept slowly by, so unlike the towering mountains situated at the extreme edges of the great plateau, remembered from just a few days past. He knew that they would make an overnight stop somewhere in eastern Alberta and complete the journey tomorrow.

The seventies sped by swiftly. John did not realize at the time that, like sands through the hourglass, so passed the summer of his life. He was determined that he would one day become a rodeo rider. In his seventeenth summer he traveled with a friend and his family to the Calgary Stampede. The feverish pace of the rodeo performers, the swirling dust, the adrenaline-fueled action and the colorful dress all had their effect upon the youth. After that visit he was certain. There could be no doubt. In spite of all the pleading on his mother's part and the cajoling and threatening on his father's part, he left in the summer of his eighteenth year to seek his fortune. As Horace Greeley had said, "Go west, young man, go west."

Jack suddenly realized that the tune issuing from the tape deck was different. The melancholy strains of a crying fiddle came forth as he heard George Jones offer his rendering of the hit song "Choices." This was music that he loved, and he settled back to take it all in. He knew that life, in spite of its promise of great things to come, was inherently sad, and the music put it all in perspective. He thought about his own choices, the times when he had taken a path of his own choosing in spite of contradictory advice from others, the first turning in the road, now so many years behind. He knew that one aspect of so-called growing up was that dreams and fantasy became reality. Childhood dreams could be cast aside with no regrets if they did not live up to expectations. When adult dreams came to fruition, they often carried their own baggage in the form of consequences.

To eighteen-year-old John, the Star Cross Ranch on the eastern slope of the Rockies in southern Alberta was heaven indeed. He had landed the job through a friend, Willie Jones, one of the few black cowboys in the region. He had met Willie at the stampede the year before. His keen desire to learn and his love of working with cattle and horses made his rapid advancement in the business all but certain. Willie was only four years older than John and they developed a lasting friendship, made all the greater when Willie introduced John to the rodeo circuit two years later. Jerry was also employed at the ranch, hiring on just a few weeks after John, and before long the threesome became inseparable. Where one could be found, the other two would not be far behind.

John had proven his riding abilities in the short time that he had been employed at the Star Cross. Gifted with a keen mind, and quick to try and learn the aspects of ranching, he rapidly came to the attention of the ranch owner, Horace Abernathy. Always looking for ways to promote his large cattle empire, Horace encouraged a select few of his cowboys to work the rodeo circuit, to advertise the caliber of the Star Cross employees. John's

JACK'S JOURNEY

abilities earned him a place on the circuit, locally at first, then on to greater things. Although he had never won the really big competitions, he made a good showing, supplementing his ranch earnings with a tidy sum in prize money won over the years.

The setting sun was sinking low in the rearview mirror when Jerry turned the pickup in to the driveway of a roadside motel. After registering for one night, he moved the truck to the space in front of the motel room. Walking around the vehicle and opening the passenger door, he assisted Jack into the room and eased him onto the second bed. Jerry walked to the window and stared at the afterglow on the western horizon for some minutes, deep in thought. Sighing, he closed the curtains, locked the door and went out to seek his supper at the nearby restaurant.

Jack lay back on his bed. Odd that he was not at all hungry. He probably would not be able to sleep either. Oh well, everything in its time. Funny how his thoughts kept returning to that road traveled long ago, a road with a vivid memory for every mile.

Jack stood with his back to the bar, his hat pushed back on his head, a tomato juice in his right hand, his boot heel hooked on the foot rail and his left elbow resting on the dark wooden surface. He always made it a point to abstain from booze the night before a performance. There would always be the night after to make up for it.

His attention wandered to the departing view of the voluptuous barmaid as she carried her heavily laden tray to the far end of the room. A pang of desire stirred within him, yet he recalled that lately his thinking had undergone a change — why, he did not know. Perhaps it was middle age, but he had begun to think more often about settling down. He had become weary of the whole scene, the faded glamour of life on the road and the one-night stands. He thought of his parents and the settled life

165

they had enjoyed on that peaceful Manitoba farm, the comfortable routine and the faith that tomorrow would be as good as or better than today. The last couple of times that Jack had been in touch with them, they had mentioned the possibility of retirement. They had hinted strongly that they wished Jack would take over the family enterprise. He surprised himself by thinking that maybe he would take them up on that offer; perhaps he would find someone to share his hopes and dreams, someone who could add some meaning to his life. Maybe this would be his last year on the circuit.

Jerry and Willie were hunched forward on their bar stools, clutching their beers, deep in conversation. Joining in the dialogue was a stranger, a local fellow by the look of him, dressed in the working duds of a Cariboo cowboy — misshapen hat, plaid shirt, Levis and a well-worn pair of boots. He took a sip from his drink, cleared his throat and began, "I tell you, that horse is a demon. You can't mistake him when you see him, black as midnight with a heart to match. Spirit Dancer they call him 'cause he'll dance on your grave given half a chance. Nobody has ridden him for the full count yet, and if you have the misfortune to draw him, you had better be prepared to exit the arena when you get throwed. He'll turn on you and stomp you if he can. At last count you could tally several broken bones, and he's been responsible for more bruises than you can count. I'm not afraid to admit that I would just as soon stay away from that killer. Many an old-timer I've talked to has said that there never was a horse like that one around these parts before."

Jack's attention was diverted back to the conversation at the bar by this last comment. He would be the only one of the trio to ride in tomorrow's performance. As this was a small, local rodeo Jerry and Willie were not participating. They had accompanied Jack to offer their moral support. Perhaps they would ride as pickup when Jack made his run.

The dawn was still only a faint promise in the eastern sky when Jerry roused from his slumber. Opting for a later breakfast stop some miles down the road, they began the second day of the journey. The rising sun found them a few miles from the Saskatchewan border.

Jerry had just stepped on the accelerator to pass a slow-moving vehicle when the engine of his pickup began to cough and lose power. Quickly pulling off to the shoulder of the road, he jumped out of the cab and raised the hood, quickly deducing that the problem was a plugged fuel filter. "Thank goodness for modern technology," he thought as he dialed the number of the automobile association on his cell phone. The operator, in turn, directed him to the local towing service, and they were soon on their way, losing only about four hours from their schedule.

The rest of the day passed quickly, the miles falling behind. Suppertime brought them near the Manitoba border. A couple of hours more would see them to their destination. Once again Jack's thoughts turned inwards, and the pictures in his memory marched along.

"This isn't a big rodeo as rodeos go," Jack thought as he eyed the crowd. He had certainly seen much larger crowds in his travels. "Oh well," he thought. He had decided to enter only the saddle bronc event here, just to keep his hand in, a sort of side venture from the fishing trip that they had originally planned at the nearby lakes. The end of the rodeo season was at hand and this would make a fitting exit.

Saturday had dawned crystal clear. As the trio made their way to the rodeo arena, Jack gazed out the open passenger window of the pickup, seeing the flat of the great plateau, reminding him of the flatness of the prairie of his youth. The majesty of the distant snowcapped mountains was lost to him at this moment. His mind registered only that which was locked so securely within his memory; that recollection so fondly remembered, which had lately begun to weigh upon his thoughts.

"Ladies and gentlemen, cowgirls and buckaroos," began the rodeo announcer, "we will now begin the bucking horse event."

Jack was brought swiftly back to reality when he realized that the announcer had just called the assignments for the bucking event. Out of twelve horses, he had drawn number seven, Spirit Dancer. After the conversation at the bar the previous night, he had some apprehension about this turn of the card. He would have to make the best of it. At worst it would be a short ride, a jarring fall and a bruise or two to nurse in the coming weeks, something to yarn about on an evening of a long winter's day.

The last fifty miles of the journey were at hand. The Ford pickup seemed to move with a purpose, alone on this secondary road, fleeing from the purple afterglow of a breathtaking prairie sunset towards the rising disc of a gigantic golden moon. Jerry began to watch for landmarks that had been pointed out by a fellow at a service station a few miles back. As this was his first visit here, he had felt the need to ask for directions. Finally he spied the tall communications tower that had been mentioned by the service station attendant. The driveway to the Slade farm should be a quarter mile beyond, on the right.

"Almost there," thought Jack. It would be good to rest. The last few days had been hectic, to say the least. Funny, how things always came at you unexpected like.

Jack eased himself down onto the horse's back. He could feel the mighty animal quivering as he stood in the chute. The horse was not overly big, but he was muscular, black and fast. The eyes rolled at times, seeming to burn with a fire within. Jack shivered slightly with a feeling of dread just before the gate was opened and the fury exploded from the chute. He knew immediately that he was in for the ride of his life.

Spirit Dancer knew every trick in the book and a few more besides, twisting and turning at the same time as he arched his back, landing hard on stiff forelegs, head down, trying to pitch his rider forward. Finally, after what seemed an eternity, Jack knew that he had won. The eight-second count had just ended and the pickup crew was moving in. Suddenly the horse veered right, toward the fence, intent on crushing Jack's leg against the rail. Jack flipped his right foot out of the stirrup. As though he had been waiting for this move, Spirit Dancer reared up on his hind legs and twisted savagely around to his left. Jack lost control and tumbled from the horse's back. The horse continued his turn, and as Jack hit the earth the hooves struck savagely down. A brilliant light erupted in the rider's brain and then the night descended. Jack saw no more. He did not see the hind legs of the horse rear up and strike Willie's palomino squarely in the chest, knocking him off his feet. He did not see Jerry's big bay collide with Spirit Dancer as he was off balance. He did not hear the crack of the rogue stallion's hind leg as the horse fell heavily, breaking it. He did not feel himself being pulled under the lower corral rail and out of the ring by Willie, who was also dragging a broken leg behind him. And he did not see the grizzled old cowboy walk into the arena with his carbine to put the wildly thrashing horse out of his misery and send him to that faraway range where the sun never sets and he could run free as the wind.

Dimly Jack remembered waking in a strange room, a room of soft pastel colors and white sheets. He remembered the voice of the doctor saying, "He's suffered a bad concussion. We'll have to watch him closely for a few days, but he should make a full recovery."

Jerry turned the pickup in to the gravel driveway. He saw that the porch light was already on, as were the interior lights of the rambling farmhouse. It was all as he had heard Jack describe it many times, a neat, peaceful setting, and good to come home to at the end of the day.

Jerry hesitated before getting out of the truck. He saw the door to the house open and a man and a woman step outside. Jerry walked around to the passenger door of the truck. Opening it he reached inside and picked up the velvet-covered box that sat on the seat. He looked at it for a few moments. On top of the box was mounted a large silver buckle. He could read the words by the soft light of the pickup's interior light. *John Emerson Slade, 1963-2001, always a contender.* Slowly he turned, walked towards the anxious couple on the porch and set the box into the woman's waiting arms. The tears trickled down her cheeks.

"I don't know what to say, Miz Slade. When I phoned you four days ago, it was the hardest job I ever had to do. The doctor said it was a blood clot in the brain. They missed it somehow. I think, though, that Jack had a feeling that all would not be well. Even I didn't know that while he was in the hospital he had written down all his plans for the eventuality that something like this could happen. The letter was in his effects, addressed to me, left with instructions that I should receive it. When I visited with him in the hospital, all he said was that he was getting tired and he would like to go home."

Myrna Slade wept quietly, holding her son's ashes lovingly in her arms. Walter Slade's hand rested tenderly on her shoulder.

"There was one more thing Jack instructed me to do." Jerry handed her a sealed letter. "I was to give you this letter. I don't know what it is. He never told me."

JACK'S JOURNEY

With trembling hands she opened the letter. By the light of the overhead porch light she read it.

> I'll say farewell yet not goodbye
> but just until another time,
> when all then need not wonder why
> so steep these hills that we must climb.
>
> To seek, to search, yet seldom find
> a port secure from any blow,
> a place so dear now comes to mind
> with a warm, west breeze so soft and slow.
>
> But place me now upon this earth,
> though with many things still left unsaid.
> I will rest in this land that gave me birth
> with a carpet of wildflowers for my bed.
>
> With a golden moon to light the path
> though I never more will roam.
> The journey now all done at last
> and I'll be forever home.

The poem was signed *John Emerson Slade.*

The peace of the night was disturbed only by the quiet sobs. The slumbering land stretched towards eternity, the shadows etched into the landscape by a gigantic prairie moon.

"It's good to be home," thought Jack. Soon he would rest.

THE BELLS OF SAINT AUBIN

"The land lay empty, peopled only by ghosts from a distant past."

This line of text, remembered from some long-forgotten book he had read, popped into Steve's mind. How it fit the scene before his eyes: a straight two-lane blacktop road leading to a vanishing point on the distant horizon, bordered on both sides by seemingly endless fields of green, dotted here and there with small copses of poplar and occasional spruce, a sky of the most brilliant blue overhead, and not a house or any other building in sight. For the moment it felt like he was the only living being on this earth. There was not even an errant bird or a contrail from a passing jet airplane in his field of vision.

This journey had been a whim, an impulse to return to a place he had left so long ago. He had never been back, not even for a short visit, yet somehow he had never forgotten his early roots.

Stephen Acheson was sixty-seven years of age, retired for the last two of those years. Having lived the past fifty-five years in Ontario, he had often thought about revisiting this place of his early memories, but he had known for some time that there would be little left here that would connect to his early childhood. In his occasional travels through the prairie regions, he had not ventured the couple of hundred miles off the main routes required to reach this out-of-the-way area. Now that he was retired he thought that he should, once more, lay eyes on the place of his birth before he passed into that great beyond.

"Saint Aubin" was a name that conjured memories in Steve's

mind. It had been a small town as prairie towns go, home to a couple of hundred people at best, boasting a once-a-week railroad, a grain elevator, a school, two small churches and a few struggling businesses. It had once been the big world to him, but now, he supposed, it would only be a memory because of the changes in the countryside. The town had lain on the upper reaches of a shallow valley, a low area in a vast flat plain. The farm where Steve had spent his early years had been a mile away from the town limits, within the valley itself. A river had flowed in the trough of the valley, which had been formed by glacial action thousands of years before.

The land within the valley itself was rather marginal. About thirty-five years earlier, someone had gotten the idea that a dam should be built, both for irrigation and limited power production. This had been done, and the old farm that he so dearly remembered now lay beneath the surface of a lake, about two miles wide and twenty miles long. He could never remember the name given to this lake, but someone had told him in passing that the locals referred to it as "The Big Pond."

The town of Saint Aubin had, apparently, passed into history. The surrounding farmland had been acquired by a couple of very large farming operations whose owners lived many miles away. The road through Saint Aubin no longer led anywhere except into the lake itself. The settlement had slowly withered away. The town, he knew, was situated about three miles north of the road that he was traveling on, about seven miles ahead.

The sun had passed the highest point in the sky on this glorious June day when Steve spied a crossroads ahead. The gravel road leading off to the right was, he knew from his map, the one that led to the site of Saint Aubin and the lake beyond. The road to the left, which was paved, intersected a much more traveled route about four miles distant. A small service station and store sat nestled near the crossroads. Judging by the modern appearance of everything, he guessed that the building was not more than two or three years old. Glancing at his gas gauge, Steve decided to stop at the service station before making his way to the old town site.

"Fill her up, mister?" queried the middle-aged attendant as he adjusted his John Deere cap slightly higher upon a balding pate.

"By all means," replied Steve, surprised at the full service, which was becoming more rare. "By the way, do you sell coffee?"

An answer in the affirmative caused Steve to reach across the seat, pick up his vacuum bottle and follow the service attendant into the station after his gas tank had been filled.

After filling up the vacuum bottle with coffee, black, no sugar or cream, and paying the man for the gas and coffee, Steve hesitated for a moment and then asked, "I'm on my way to Saint Aubin. I haven't been there for a number of years. What can you tell me about the place? Is anything left of the town?"

The service station attendant gathered his thoughts. Raising his cap with his right hand, he absently scratched his head before he replied, "Well, I've only been here three years myself. Moved up to get away from the rat race in the city. The road you came in on doesn't see all that much traffic, but the road from the west and the connector to the highway south of here are usually fairly busy. I realized there would be a good opportunity to set up a business of this sort here. Not much left of the town except the old hotel and a few other buildings. Can't even see it from here unless you know about it, as it sets just over the rim of the valley. The store closed its doors about four years ago. That was when I got the idea for this place."

Steve's mind digested the offered information before he asked the fellow another question. "I guess nobody lives there now?"

"You got that right, although one old lady, Mrs. Thistlewaite, lived there until she passed away early this year. She owned the old hotel in town for about sixty years from what I understand, along with her husband, Harry. Almost to the end she made a show of keeping the place clean, as though she expected business to pick up again. I had coffee with her a couple of times on the veranda of the hotel. Clean as a whistle it was. You could eat off the floor."

Instant recognition of that name flashed through Steve's thoughts as he recalled the woman and her husband, who would have been around thirty years of age some fifty-five years before. "I wonder how she managed to live here after the town declined. Surely it would cost money to keep up the hotel."

"Money was not a problem. Harry, although he's been gone for twenty years or more, was related, so I've been told, to the Thistlewaite family that is one of two major landowners in this area. He had owned much of the land at the time the dam was built. His wife sold out her share of the farming interests after his death. She loved this town and chose to live on at the old hotel. She was a pleasant person, although a bit of a recluse in her later years."

The conversation continued, covering the topics of crops, weather and whatever else of interest came up. Steve thanked the fellow and returned to his car.

Steve tooled the car slowly along the rutted gravel road. The man at the service station had mentioned that as the land in this area was largely controlled by a couple of families, and because there really was nowhere to go beyond Saint Aubin, few people entered here. Road maintenance was almost non-existent. As the car dipped over the lip of the escarpment, a small collection of

THE BELLS OF ST. AUBIN

weathered buildings came into Steve's view. A two-story frame building stood about halfway along the block, on the right. He could see at a glance that it had been painted sometime within the last few years. That, he knew from memory, would be the Aubin Hotel. The rest of the old buildings bore a dilapidated appearance, not having seen paint in many, many years.

As he cruised along the rough roadway, he read the text barely visible on the sign in front of a building to his left. *J. Harris, Groceries and Meats*. This was not a name he remembered from his childhood, so he could only assume that the store had changed hands at some point. Next door to the grocery store stood the remains of an old service station. The single bay door hung crookedly, leaving the interior of the place open to the weather. In front of the station stood the skeletons of a pair of ancient gas pumps, the type that had a glass reservoir above the pumps. The gas had to be pumped by hand into these reservoirs before being fed by gravity into the tank of a customer's car. The glass was gone. Only the metal remained.

He drove to the far end of the street, almost to the edge of the reservoir. About a third of the town, if memory served him correctly, lay beneath those waters. At least, it did in his mind, as he was fairly certain that the buildings in that section would have been torn down before the reservoir had been created. He paused for a few moments to look out over the lake, then turned his car about and drove back to the hotel. He was certain that no one would complain if he parked on the left side. Opening the car door, he stepped outside and looked around him.

The Aubin Hotel looked much as he remembered it: a two-story building with a long veranda on the front. At one end of the veranda was a door that led into the beer parlor. At the other end, to his right, was an entrance to the restaurant portion of the building. Above this door hung a small neon sign that said sim-

177

ply *Restaurant*. It was obvious that it hadn't been illuminated for some time. Immediately ahead of him was the door into the lobby. The windows on either side of the door seemed to hide their secrets in the gloom of the shadowed interior. The rooms were on the second floor, and it was at this level, across the front of the building, that the sign was located which stated *Aubin Hotel*. A wooden handrail ran along the leading edge of the veranda, curving downward at either edge of the steps.

Climbing the three steps to the veranda, Steve noticed that everything was still in surprisingly good condition, although every surface was overlaid with a thin coat of dust. He saw, near the right end of the veranda, a small table and two chairs. Walking over to the table, he spied a sheet of paper fastened to the tabletop with several thumbtacks. On closer inspection he realized hat the paper had been laminated, covered in plastic to protect it against the weather. Looking closely, he saw that there was text on its surface. Leaning over slightly, he read:

Welcome stranger to these premises. Sit a while and take your ease. I can no longer offer you hospitality, but I can offer a short respite. Take this time to look about you. The empty buildings, the vacant streets or the silence that encompasses all do not adequately present this community as it was. From the prairie it sprang so many years ago. To the prairie it will return in its own time. All that will remain are memories. Glean some of these memories to take with you to wherever you may live so that you may recall that this was a vibrant community, full of life, laughter and the joy of being. Above all, listen to the song of the chimes, for the song of the chimes is sung by the wind, and it is the wind that is the true voice of the prairie. Even though the town will pass away, the wind will always be. It, and it alone, will tell you all there is to know.

The Bells of St. Aubin

Steve felt mistiness come into his eyes as he straightened up. Mrs. Thistlewaite had obviously left this note, probably when she realized she was failing. As he stood there, deep in thought, he felt a breath of wind upon his cheek, and the musical note of a single chime intruded on his consciousness.

With a sense of déjà vu he turned to look at the far end of the veranda. Another musical note gently caressed his senses. There above the handrail, suspended from the edge of the roof above the veranda, was a set of wind chimes. They comprised five tubular chimes of varying lengths, each measuring about an inch in diameter. They appeared to be very old, although he could see that the entire apparatus had been restrung in recent years. The heavy metal clapper hung in the center of the metal tubes and was struck alternately by the various tuned tubes as they moved to a cadence caused by the vagary of the prairie wind. A metal canopy hung over all. In the canopy was a big dent. A smile of recognition beamed across Steve's face, and in that instant he remembered.

This bright June morning in 1947 had a special meaning for young Stephen Acheson as he scrubbed his hands and face in the metal washbasin on the covered porch. Toweling off quickly, he hustled himself into the kitchen where the tantalizing smell of bacon and eggs filled the room. Not only was this the first day of the summer holiday, but he was also going to town with his mom and dad. As this was Saturday, he knew that they would spend several hours in town while his mother and father did their weekly shopping and also tried to get a bit of visiting done. Impatiently he finished his breakfast and hurried out the door, where he paced back and forth, wondering what was holding things up. After what seemed an eternity, Mom and Dad walked outside and got into the ancient Dodge car. With Stephen in the back seat they started off for town. It was only a mile, but time dragged until they passed the grain elevator on the near edge of town.

An hour and a half quickly passed while most of the required purchases were made. Mother then elected to visit a lady friend of hers, leaving Stephen and his father to their own devices. Dad's business, however, was not quite finished and he drove over to the blacksmith shop. Opening the trunk with a little difficulty, as it stuck sometimes, he removed a pair of plowshares. He and Stephen entered the smithy.

Bill Adams, standing over the forge with a pair of tongs in his hand, represented perfectly the image of a blacksmith with his sleeveless shirt, bulging arms and a trickle of sweat running down his cheek.

"Morning, Dan," he offered to Stephen's father. "I'll be with you in a second." Removing a small piece of red-hot iron from the forge, he laid it upon the anvil, beat on it with his hammer, eyed it critically and dropped it into a tub of water near one wall of the shop.

Bill and Dan shook hands and then the smith inspected the plowshares before he placed them into the glowing center of the forge.

"I'll have them ready in no time. Maybe the young fellow could turn the handle on the blower for me. It'll speed things up considerably."

Stephen quickly grabbed the handle of the blower fan and began to turn. Bill and Dan carried on their conversation while Bill worked. In a short time the job was completed, Dan paid for the work, and then he and Stephen returned to the car. Stephen grinned proudly at having been able to assist in the work at hand, but secretly he was happy that the job was done. Turning that blower fan was hard work.

The next stop would be the Aubin Hotel. Mother would not be ready to go home for another hour or so. Dad always used this time to stop at the beer parlor for one beer and a chance to talk to

THE BELLS OF ST. AUBIN

some of his farming friends. Stephen, on the other hand, was not allowed in the bar. He would spend his hour sitting at the table on the veranda with a treasured bottle of Wynola pop. He always tried to make that bottle of pop last for as long as he could.

Stephen was quietly sitting on the veranda, watching the customers coming and going to the grocery store across the street. A stiff breeze sprang up and a musical melody of bells filled his ears. Looking around, he saw something hanging from an overhead beam near the far end of the veranda. It had not been there before, and he was instantly curious, eager to determine just what it was. Leaving his half-finished pop on the table, he walked over to the device and reached up to steady the swinging object. It was almost out of his reach, so he took hold of the corner of the building at the end of the veranda and climbed onto the handrail. Taking hold of one metal tube, he attempted to examine the object. As he leaned forward for a better look, his foot slipped off the railing. With an unholy clatter, Stephen, his dignity and the wind chimes came crashing to the floor of the veranda. His face turned crimson from embarrassment as Stephen quickly picked himself off the floor while several people rushed out from the beer parlor and the hotel lobby to see what caused that tumultuous noise. Mrs. Thistlewaite, the owner, did not seem overly concerned about the wind chimes and anxiously made certain that Stephen had not been hurt. Stephen's dad inspected the chimes and, after noticing a large dent in the canopy, offered to get them repaired. Mrs. Thistlewaite declined, insisting that the dent would not hurt the chimes at all. They would simply be re-hung.

With a sense of awe, Steve gazed at the ancient wind chimes when he realized that they had hung there for nearly fifty-eight years.

For a few moments Steve stood staring at the chimes, mesmerized by the sudden rush of memory they had invoked within

SHADOWS IN THE WIND

him. Reluctantly he turned away, pausing to cast a wandering glance over the scattered remains of this town that had been a part of his life those many years ago, fully aware that when he left this place today, he would never return. He would take the advice of the lady who had written the note on the tabletop at the far end of the veranda. He would glean these memories and he would take them away.

Steve returned to his car, parked near the foot of the steps. Removing the vacuum flask of coffee, he carried it around to the back of his car, where he retrieved a bottle of rye whiskey from the trunk. Pouring a generous measure of the rye into the not-quite-full coffee container, he returned to the small table on the veranda. After filling his cup to the brim, he pulled up a chair, took a sip and prepared to spend a relaxing time reminiscing. He knew that his room for the night, booked in advance at a town about thirty minutes away, would be waiting for him whenever he chose to arrive there. A couple or three drinks would be long worn off before he would be ready to leave here. Supper would present no problem as he carried a small cooler in his car trunk. The cooler was packed with cold cuts, bread, butter, fruit and other food.

The alcohol in his coffee served to mellow Steve's mood even more than it had been calmed by the inrush of pleasant memories. The overhead sun in an almost cloudless sky and the encompassing silence of the land, a silence broken only by the occasional, nearly inaudible, sigh of a prairie breeze, served to accentuate his longing for a time so very distant. Taking another soothing swallow from his cup, he gazed to the west along the rim of the shallow valley, which flaunted the varied colors of the wildflowers and the greens of the trees and grasses as it reached towards the edge of that inverted great blue bowl that was the sky.

The names of the nearby streets made their way into Steve's

THE BELLS OF ST. AUBIN

consciousness as he turned his attention once more to the layout of the town before him. The street running from south to north, on which he had arrived from the service station at the crossroads, was the one directly in front of him, Main Street. The next street to the west was Poplar Street. On the far side of this street he could see the old Roman Catholic Church and the United Church, side by side, with their front entrances facing where he sat. A couple of vacant lots and several old houses of varying sizes and descriptions flanked them. The near side of Poplar Street showed only the rear view of a pair of nondescript structures, the odd pile of rubble and three vacant lots. Many of the old buildings had disappeared with time.

At the intersection to the right of where Steve took his ease, running east to west, was Elmer Avenue, and one block to the north, also running east to west, was Railway Avenue. The corner of Elmer Avenue and Poplar Street, just to the north and west of the intersection, had been home to the community hall. The corner of Poplar Street and Railway Avenue, across the avenue from the onetime railroad track, was the location of the blacksmith shop. Just beyond the intersection of Main Street and Railway Avenue, parallel to Railway Avenue, was what remained of the old railroad grade. The grain elevator had been located just north and west of the intersection of Railway Avenue and Main Street. The farm that had been Steve's home was located slightly more than a mile beyond the elevator and was now beneath the shimmering blue water, inaccessible except perhaps to the fish. Both the elevator and the railroad tracks had vanished into history many years before.

Looking back to his left, he could see that the south end of Poplar Street ended at a large wrought-iron gate. Beyond this gate, just past the edge of the town, was the cemetery. This cemetery, he recalled, had been shared by all who lived in the area,

SHADOWS IN THE WIND

regardless of denomination.

Leisurely draining the remains of his coffee cup, Steve placed it on the tabletop and rose to his feet. A stroll around the town site was in order. As he started north from the hotel stairs towards the intersection of Main Street and Elmer Avenue, he saw that the old municipal office building, immediately adjacent to the hotel, still stood, looking forlorn. No markings showed upon its exterior. Several of the windows were broken, and the *Municipal Hall* sign that had once graced the front wall had been removed, leaving little indication that this building had once housed the driving force behind the small community.

Turning west on Elmer, Steve arrived at the next intersection, Elmer and Poplar. He stopped for a moment to gaze towards the cemetery at the south end of Poplar Street. He noticed that the stained glass in the windows of the two churches was still largely intact. A single gust of wind caused a pane of glass, loosened with age, to flutter in the window of the Roman Catholic Church. A brief flash of brilliance caused by the glass's momentary shifting in the afternoon sun caught his attention. A single peal of the wind chimes sounded from the veranda of the nearby hotel, sounding ever so fleetingly like a church bell. In an instant he was carried back to the time, so long ago, when he had accompanied his mother and father to that church almost every Sunday.

Stephen Acheson tried not to attract attention as he unobtrusively loosened the tight-fitting collar on his white shirt. This bright July morning of 1947 promised to be very warm by midday. He couldn't wait for Sunday mass to be over so he could change into his overalls again. The priest had not yet begun, and the sound of church bells filled the air. Stephen looked about him. His mother and father sat to his right, looking ahead, patiently waiting for the mass to begin. Mr. Devers, the railroad station agent, sat in the pew ahead of them. Stephen could see that Mr. Devers, a bit on the portly side and appearing less than comfortable in his black suit, had nodded off. His eyes were closed although he sat stiffly upright.

Glancing to one side, Stephen noticed that Nancy Smith sat beside her parents near the far side of the church. She was a classmate of Stephen and the same age as him. Although he would never admit it, he found himself attracted to her. She noticed his glance and shyly smiled. Stephen quickly turned to look toward the front of the church again, his face turning a slight shade of crimson.

Slowly, although to Stephen it seemed forever, the church filled and the priest slowly made his way to the altar. A feeling of peace settled over Stephen, like a comforting blanket on a cool winter's day. The rays of the morning sun penetrated the stained glass windows, highlighting the dust motes as they danced about in the golden sunbeams.

Funny, thought Stephen, how Sunday mornings always seemed so much brighter than other weekdays. On Sundays it felt like all things would be well.

Steve's mind quickly returned to the present. How small the church looked. The entrance door still hung in its frame, although he could see a definite sag on one side, making it appear to bow beneath the weight of the years, much as he himself was now doing. The old church looked merely empty. All, even the memories, had gone home.

Making his way along, Steve noticed an old house set well back from the street. It was two stories in height with a roofline that showed no sag even after the passage of the decades. In the front yard stood a large crab apple tree. Steve saw the newly formed fruit upon the tree even as he recalled the lady who had lived here when he had been a boy. Mrs. Corbett was the name that came to mind. She, like the old house, had stood straight and

SHADOWS IN THE WIND

upright despite her seventy years of age, always with an air of authority about her. She had lived here for many years with a dog called Brutus.

Steve's steps had carried him to the gate of the cemetery. He saw that the wrought-iron gate was open just far enough for him to enter. As he looked about, he spied a fairly recent mound of earth near the entrance. Crossing over to the gravesite, he saw that the marker had not yet been placed. A temporary marker had been set into a now faded wreath on the ground. The words on the marker said simply *Amanda Thistlewaite 1921–2005*. On the grave alongside was a faded headstone with the words *Harry Thistlewaite 1919–1986*. For a few moments Steve stood with his head bowed, trying to recall the faces of these people who had left their mark upon the land so many years ago. Raising his eyes once again after a few moments of contemplation, Steve walked on.

The names on the headstones seemed to leap into Steve's consciousness as he recognized many, although not all, of the inscriptions. A large ornate stone offered the name of *TOWERS Chadwick Owen 1899–1966*. Mr. Towers, Steve recalled, had been the principal of the school here at Saint Aubin all those many years ago. The name and the large stone tended to conjure up an image of a large man, yet Steve remembered that Mr. Towers had stood no more than five foot seven, although to a young Stephen Acheson he had loomed very large indeed, especially on the one or two occasions when Stephen had been on the receiving end of the strap wielded by the principal. No resentment lingered in Steve's memories. It had been the way of the times. Discipline and compassion had shared equal billing on that giant motion-picture screen called life.

A sudden fluttering of the prairie wind set the wind chimes in motion, sounding for all the world, even if they were slightly mut-

THE BELLS OF ST. AUBIN

ed by the intervening distance, like a school bell calling everyone back to those long-ago halls of learning. In their time they had come, they had learned, they had departed, and the school bell would never call again.

Farther along, Steve came to a grouping of three graves. Two names, Marie and Maurice Ducharme, triggered a recollection of the old grocery store. These people had been the owners when Steve was but a lad. It was the third grave of the trio that unleashed vivid memories hidden deep in Steve's mind. *August Ducharme 1937–1959* imprinted itself on Steve's thoughts. He had been the son of the owners of the grocery store. He had also been a friend of young Stephen Acheson. Steve recalled him as a rather rambunctious, fun-loving individual, slightly unpredictable, living for the moment and never one to harbor a grudge. Steve had lost touch with Augie Ducharme when the Acheson family moved east in 1950. Some years later Steve learned from another friend that Augie had died, a victim of demon rum it was said. In reality, Steve now knew, Augie had been killed in a car accident while returning home after overdoing it on moonshine at a local dance. Once again, a feeling of nostalgia overcame Steve and the years flowed away.

A bright August full moon hung over the small town of Saint Aubin on this evening of 1946. Stephen Acheson's mother and father were attending a social evening at the local community hall. Stephen had been with them earlier for the supper, but after the meal he had quickly joined forces with his friend Augie. Quickly becoming bored with the activities of the adults, as boys of eight or nine are wont to do, they wandered outside to explore the magic of the moonlit prairie night. They stood for a few moments to plot a strategy to amuse them as they stood outside the community hall and looked to the south along Poplar Street.

"How would you like some nice crab apples, Steve?" quipped

Augie. "I saw that the tree at Mrs. Corbett's was loaded when I walked by this afternoon."

"I don't know," replied Stephen. "You know she has that huge dog, Brutus. I've never known him to bite anyone, but he sure raises a ruckus whenever anyone comes by the fence."

"Ah, that's okay. She keeps him in the house at this time of night. We'll be very careful. He won't even know we're there."

Stealthily the two boys made their way along the street. As the small gate was padlocked, they chose to climb over the picket fence. As they approached the crab apple tree, Augie stooped to cup his hands and give Stephen a boost up to where the inviting fruit hung upon the sagging limbs. Stephen secured his position in the tree branches and began to pick apples, stuffing them into his shirtfront as he did so. For the moment, silence filled the velvet darkness.

The boys suddenly heard an ominous "click" as the front door of the house was unlatched. A furious barking filled the night.

"Run" was the only word Augie shouted as he tore off into the night. Stephen stumbled from his precarious perch and followed quickly in pursuit. The barking of the dog, Brutus, was increasing in volume. With a single leap, Augie cleared the picket fence. Stephen, overloaded with the crab apples, tried to copy him. He stumbled and fell. Brutus was upon him. A momentary image of slashing canine teeth filled Stephen's mind as the dog's face descended toward his own. Instead of the ripping of fangs, though, Stephen's face was covered by great, slobbering licks. After what seemed an eternity, yet was only a few seconds, Stephen picked himself up off the ground, trying, with some difficulty, to distance himself from the dog. He stumbled to the fence, losing his hard-won gains in the process as the crab apples spilled upon the ground. Vaulting over, he ran in pursuit of Augie, with the

THE BELLS OF ST. AUBIN

diminishing sound of the dog's barking following in his wake.

The funny part about that long-ago recollection, Steve remembered, was that he had heard no mention of the occurrence afterward, although he detected a rather smug expression on the face of Mrs. Corbett on the next couple of occasions that he met her.

Steve continued on his circuit of the cemetery. He realized that most of the headstones here were many years old. This place had seen little activity in some time. The plot in which Mrs. Thistlewaite was buried would probably be the last. The town itself would "return to the prairie" as the note on the hotel veranda had said. The seasons would come and go. The prairie wind would continue to sing its mournful song, but no one would be around to hear. Time, for Steve, seemed to pause momentarily. The fragrance of the tiger lilies filled the clear afternoon air. The plaintive call of a songbird drifted across the meadows. What kind of bird it was he did not know. He had been too long in the city.

Steve studied the name on the next headstone for a few moments. *Roger Minton* rang a bell in Steve's memory. The date on the stone, *1932–1953*, with a raised bugle above it provided the clue. Roger had attended the school at Saint Aubin, but he had been in a class several years ahead of Stephen Acheson. Roger had finished his schooling in 1949. He had then enlisted in the army. Steve had heard from someone in passing that Roger had gone to Korea. The wings of an errant bullet had found him, now the prairie claimed him as its own.

Coming to the farthest edge of the cemetery, Steve saw two relatively plain stone markers. They stood upright, side by side, about two and a half feet in height. The stone on the right bore a simple cross on the upper portion, with the text *Jean Adams 1912–1987*. The stone on the left showed *Bill Adams 1905–1978*. This stone too bore a cross, although this one was slightly larger and was composed of a blacksmith's hammer, standing upright, head down. The crossbar was a pair of blacksmith's tongs in the closed position. For a few moments Steve stood transfixed, a catch in his throat. He suddenly realized that the work of the blacksmith was done and the tools were forever at rest. A lilting breeze sprang up on the prairie, and the wind chimes sounded in the near distance, a lively rhythmical melody, like the cadence of the blacksmith's hammer on the surface of the anvil in tune with the measured beat of the hammer on the surface of the work in progress. But it was just for a moment. Then all was still.

Exiting the wrought-iron gate once more, Steve slowly walked along Poplar Street to where it intersected with Elmer Avenue. Turning left at the corner, he passed a couple of decrepit old buildings, not too large, definitely business premises of some sort. Straining his memory, he recalled that the third building on his left had been an insurance office. Of course in those days there was hardly enough insurance business in a small town to make a living. This insurance agent had sold farm machinery as well. A large lot was located behind the building. This was where the farm implements or an occasional tractor had been stored while awaiting delivery to their buyers. The lot was vacant now, except for an ancient, rusting, horse-drawn mower. There were weeds of every description, overgrown due to the absence of anyone to keep them trimmed — weeds and assorted bits of trash deposited over the decades by human agency, passing animals and the wind itself.

There was an empty lot across the street to Steve's right. The theater had stood here at the time he had left Saint Aubin. He realized suddenly that he could remember the last motion picture he had watched there with his mother and father early in 1950. It was *Twelve O'Clock High*, with Gregory Peck in a leading role. How thrilling it had been to watch the daring exploits of the heavy bombers and their gallant crews, especially with the real war only five years past at that time. Sixty years had come and gone since the Second World War. The theater was no more. The bombers had been grounded for decades. Silence was the order of the day. An errant gust of wind brought a single, brief response from the wind chimes in the distance. It sounded to Steve like a tribute to those bygone heroes of the silver screen, triggering in his mind a recollection of an even older movie, also viewed in this very theater, *For Whom The Bell Tolls.*

Continuing west along Elmer Avenue, Steve arrived at a small two-story house on the left side of the street. Beyond this was a large empty area. The old house, with a pronounced sag in the roofline, broken windows and a crumbling chimney at one end, was, as Steve recalled, the teacher's residence, dating back to the early days of the twentieth century. The school had been in the vacant area beyond. Even in his time here the old house had outgrown its original purpose and was used mainly for storage. The school's staff had resided elsewhere in the community. The school had been much newer and had likely been salvaged for the building material. The school, as Steve remembered, consisted of six rooms. Five had been classrooms while the sixth had been a common room, a place where activities, concerts, and other events had taken place.

As Steve stood gazing at the empty field before him, he tried to remember one event that he attended here as a child. A small dust devil sprang up on the field before him, coming from somewhere out on the prairie, dancing erratically across his vision, whirling the various bits of paper and old leaves as it made its way towards the old railroad grade. A restless breeze preceded the dust devil and, far across the expanse of the small town, muted by the distance, the wind chimes again made their presence known with a fitful, fluttering sound that reminded Steve ever so much, despite the warmth of the June afternoon, of sleigh bells.

Suddenly a memory of a distant Christmas concert sprang into his mind.

Young Stephen was almost beside himself with excitement. This was the evening of the Christmas concert, and he had been picked to portray a shepherd guarding his flock in the Christmas play that his class was presenting to the, no doubt, critical acclaim of parents and other doting members of the families scattered throughout the area. This day was December 17, 1946. Stephen was eight years old.

Opening the door a crack to see if Dad had started the car yet, Stephen noticed that there was a light snow falling. There was a definite edge to the wind as well. Oh well, he thought, it will be warm in the car. Stephen felt he was fortunate that his father owned a car, even though it was several years old. Many of the families still relied on a team of horses and a sleigh for their winter journeys into town.

The trip into town seemed to take forever as Stephen tried to see out through the increasing snowfall. The wind had picked up a bit too. Small drifts lay across the roadway. The rise and fall of the car as it struck these drifts made it feel to Stephen as though it were a ship on the bounding main. Finally the lights of the town became visible through the swirling snow. Stephen quickly forgot the storm as he bounded into the school, eager for the festivities to begin. Dan Acheson held the door open for his wife. He paused before he entered the building to cast a worried glance into the darkness.

The evening's presentation carried on without a hitch. The thunder of applause filled the room as the closing act of the Christmas play concluded. Dan Acheson hurried to the door, opening it slightly to check on the weather. He quickly noticed that the temperature had plummeted. A real blizzard was blowing. He had earlier noticed that most of the neighbors who lived some distance from town were absent. With only a mile distance to his farm from the edge of the village, he was confident they would get home, but while the bulk of the crowd tarried for coffee and goodies, he quickly bundled his family into the car and they started on their way.

As soon as the grain elevator, seen only as a hulking darkness, had been left behind, Dan Acheson realized that the one-mile journey would not be a simple feat. Swirling snow enveloped the car, challenging the capability of the headlights to show the way. The snowdrifts on the roadway were much deeper than they had been earlier, causing the car to lurch laboriously every few yards. Stephen, sitting anxiously in the rear seat, kept his gaze fastened to the darkness outside he window, trying, in vain, to see the gateposts that marked the entrance to their yard. They had gone no more than half a mile since leaving the grain elevator behind when they heard a sudden pop from the engine as the car struggled to negotiate a particularly deep drift. Clouds of steam engulfed the car, making it even more difficult to see anything outside the window.

"We've blown a radiator hose," muttered Dan to his wife, Millie, as he switched off the ignition.

"What are we going to do?" she ventured.

"We'll stay with the car. We're all warmly dressed, and if this blizzard quits blowing we can walk home. It's not more than a half mile."

Huddling beneath blankets, which had been carried in the car as an emergency precaution, they waited out the storm. Outside, the swirling blanket of snow continued its wild acrobatics. The banshee wail of the wind filled the void. Stephen, saying not a word, was certain this would be their final night on earth.

For the briefest of moments there was a lull in the melee of the storm. Stephen could only wonder. What was he hearing? It sounded like bells, sleigh bells.

"Hello the car," came a voice from out of the darkness.

Dan Acheson, straining to identify the owner of the voice, replied, "George? George Sanders?"

George was a neighbor, a farmer who lived about two miles beyond the Acheson place. Although he had no children and had not been at the concert, he had driven his horse team, with his caboose, into town earlier in the day and was only now returning home.

"Pile into the caboose," boomed the gruff voice after Dan had explained their predicament. "We'll have you home in a jiffy."

The team of horses plodded onward into the blizzard, which had returned with a vengeance. Arriving at the Acheson farm, Dan and Millie persuaded George Sanders to put his horses up in the barn and spend the night. It would be foolhardy to continue in these weather conditions.

Young Stephen Acheson curled up in his bed, never so glad to be home and warm. He drifted off to sleep with the sound of sleigh bells in his ears.

Turning right, toward the west, Steve continued along the unnamed street that intersected Railway Avenue farther on. Even those many years ago, he recalled, this street had no name, and only a couple of old granaries had occupied space along its entire length. Beyond the street was the prairie. Steve crossed Railway Avenue and turned onto the old grade itself. The tracks had been gone for many years and the surface of the grade was covered with grass and weeds. As he passed the old blacksmith shop, he saw that someone had placed a sign in the one window that was not broken. It had obviously been someone with a sense of humor, as the sign said simply *Sorry, we're closed.*

Arriving at the intersection of Main and Railway, Steve

stopped and turned to look back toward the west. The railroad grade stretched toward the horizon. He remembered looking at the tracks from this vantage point all those years before, waiting to catch the first glimpse of the steam engine as it became visible in the distance. Closing his eyes for a moment, he could see it once more in his mind's eye. A boisterous breeze slapped his cheek, and the wind chimes on the nearby veranda gave out a series of replies, sounding like the bell of the old steam engine as it shuttled the grain cars back and forth on its weekly visits. With a start, Steve opened his eyes, half-expecting to see that ancient steam engine bearing down upon him. With one more wistful glance toward the distant horizon, he walked slowly back towards the hotel.

Steve opened the trunk of his car and removed the cooler that was within. Carrying it up the steps, he placed it on the table near the end of the veranda. Setting out a sheet of paper towel, he began to prepare his evening meal. After spreading the rye bread thickly with butter, then adding a generous helping of sliced chicken, tomato, mayonnaise and a dash of pepper, he removed a bottle of spring water from the cooler and sat back to enjoy. Looking at the bottled water for a moment, he opted to pour the last cup of laced coffee from his vacuum flask instead. The sun was still some distance from the horizon, but the evening promised to be clear, with only the occasional cloud scurrying along. A gust of wind brought a single peal from the wind chimes, like a dinner bell. Dinner was served at the Aubin Hotel.

Munching away on his sandwich here in this place of old memories was pleasant, but it did not compare to the meals he remembered from his childhood on the farm. The chicken in his sandwich did not taste quite the same. Reaching back across the years, Steve conjured up a memory of what he remembered as an ordinary evening meal.

*"Wash your hands before you sit down to the table, Stephen,"
admonished his mother. Hastily Stephen hurried out to the porch,
poured a dipper full of cold water into the washbasin, splashed
his hands and face and rubbed them dry on a towel hanging from
a rack on the wall. Hurrying inside, he sat at the table and began
to fill his plate. Breaded chicken, freshly prepared by his mother
just this forenoon, new potatoes in cream, and a green salad that
had been growing in the garden only hours before. After finishing
his second helping, Stephen knew he would be back for a snack
before bedtime. Eight-year-old boys expended a lot of energy,
and fuel was needed to feed the boiler. A piece of freshly baked
apple pie, smothered in fresh cream, topped off the meal just fine.
It was time to go outside now. There were mountains to climb,
deserts to cross and villains to exterminate.*

*The land outside the door stretched toward the distant hori-
zon. A cloudbank was visible far to the south, and the colors of
the wildflowers on the slight rise of the escarpment along the
edge of the valley added a bit of contrast to the green of the fields
on an early July evening. The prairie sun, in all its glory, ruled
this domain. Nightfall was still far away.*

Glancing for a moment at the remains of the chicken sandwich on
the paper plate before him, Steve was quick to note that it certainly
did seem like the taste of chicken had changed over time, or perhaps
it was only the passing of the years that created that impression.

After completing his meal, washed down with half a bottle
of the water as well as the coffee, Steve rose from his chair. The
sun was well on its way toward the western horizon, and the front
of the hotel, facing the sun, was brightly illuminated. Walking to
the lobby entrance, Steve paused to look through the window at
the now visible interior. He could see the counter halfway across
the room where the occasional guests would sign the register so
many years ago.

THE BELLS OF ST. AUBIN

Too bad I can't go in, he thought. I'd like to see what's inside this old place.

The place would, no doubt, be locked up tight, but on a whim he reached for the doorknob and slowly turned it. The door opened at his touch. Surprised, he stood there for a few moments. An odd feeling seized him as he entered the building, as though he were entering an old, empty church. Looking around, he spied the staircase to the second floor at one end of the room. An upholstered chair sat in one corner, slightly obscured from the sunlight shining through the windows. There was no other piece of furniture in the room, not even a picture on the wall.

Glancing at the counter that he had viewed from outside, he was flabbergasted to see an open register on the surface. Beside the register was a pencil. On closer inspection he saw that the pencil had been sharpened to a fine point, as though customers were still expected. Perhaps it was the ambience of his surroundings, but he could have sworn he caught a glimpse of movement from the corner of his eye. Quickly looking toward the chair in its corner, he saw it was empty, as before. A single butterfly that had entered through the open door made one circuit of the room and departed whence it came.

Turning back to the register, Steve picked up the pencil. Concentrating deeply on the blank page before him for a few moments, he entered the text *Stephen Acheson, June 17, 2005.* Marshaling his thoughts for a minute, he wrote upon the "Address" portion of the ledger *St. Aubin.* He knew he had finally come home.

Steve settled himself into the chair at the table on the veranda of the hotel. He knew he should he going, yet he was loath to leave this place. How many memories had been awakened by this visit? Many of these memories he had thought buried so long ago. The last couple of hours quickly passed as he reminisced, watch-

SHADOWS IN THE WIND

ing the sun sink lower in the western sky, finally dipping below the horizon, leaving a glorious sky of red and eventually changing to a deep purple just before the dusk. Procrastinating to the last, Steve finally rose from the chair and prepared to leave.

With a last lingering glance around him at the shadowed silhouettes illuminated by a three-quarter prairie moon, Steve opened the car door and slid behind the wheel. Switching on the ignition, he started the engine and lowered the window on the driver's side to let in the pleasant coolness of the night air. As he slowly pulled away, the soft velvet of the night, broken only by the flicker of an occasional firefly, engulfed the little town, silent now, with memories its only inhabitants. Had there been someone to listen, they would have heard a soft sigh as the night wind moved slowly through the empty streets, a prairie wind searching in vain for something that was no longer there. A faint tinkle came from the wind chimes. The haunting call of a whippoorwill sounded briefly, and then all was silent.

As the miles sped away, Steve glanced at the illuminated clock on the dashboard. The digital readout displayed 11:30 pm. He realized that he had stayed longer than he had intended, but he knew that he would never be back and that time was of little consequence. Saint Aubin was, he mused, passing into history. The remaining buildings would slowly vanish, the victims of anyone looking for the scant material that could be salvaged. In the meantime, the prairie wind would continue to tell its story through the wind chimes there on the veranda of the old hotel. There would come a time, however, when the wire that supported the chimes would part, a casualty of the constant pressure of this same wind. The parting might come in the midst of a violent midnight thunderstorm or perhaps during a quiet moment with just a gentle August breeze lazily expounding its tales through that melodic sound, but come it would. The chimes would descend in a

THE BELLS OF ST. AUBIN

crescendo of noise, and the wind would seem to hold its breath as the sound of the wind chimes was replaced by only a soft lament. When that time came, the prairie wind would lose its voice, and the bells of Saint Aubin would ring no more.

ISBN 141209582-4

9 781412 095822